ABC OF THE CHRISTIAN LIFE

ABCs OF THE CHRISTIAN LIFE

The Ultimate Anthology of the Prince of Paradox

G. K. Chesterton
Foreword by Peter Kreeft

Christian Classics ✛ *Notre Dame, Indiana*

Paperback: ISBN-13 978-0-87061-310-4

E-book: ISBN-13 978-0-87061-311-1

Cover silhouette graphic by Katherine J. Ross.

Cover image © iStockphoto.com.

Cover and text design by Katherine Robinson.

Printed and bound in the United States of America.

Contents

Foreword

In heaven there are three people you will never confuse with anyone else because their personalities and their minds are so absolutely unique and distinctive: Jesus, Socrates, and G. K. Chesterton.

Whenever I assign Chesterton to my college students, some love him and some hate him. One student explained very candidly why he hated reading him: "His mind is a rapier, and he's dueling with me, and he cuts my clothes to ribbons and makes me feel naked and stupid." I replied: "That's exactly right. Don't you just love that?" He thought I was kidding. I told him to read Psalm 139.

Chesterton was a genius of the right hemisphere, a *seer*. He saw things we don't see; that is why we desperately need him here in the country of the blind. He seems crazy only because he is the sanest inhabitant in our global insane asylum. In an age where common sense is the uncommonest of commodities, he is the Uncommon Man. His works are the Uncommonest Manifesto.

He saw through things that we see as solid but that are really fakes and falsehoods and fallacies; and he saw solidity in things that we seem to see through but that are really solid truths and profound platitudes.

He has the reputation of tying us up in knots, but this is exactly wrong, for he is only untying the knots we have tied ourselves into. He has the reputation of being a paradox-mongerer, but this is exactly wrong, for he is only showing us the simple truth, like the little boy in "The Emperor's New Clothes." He shows us that what seems to us outrageously paradoxical is in fact simple truth, and what we see as simple truth is in fact outrageously paradoxical. *That's* the real paradox.

He has the reputation of playing games with us and constantly turning us upside down, but this is exactly wrong because he is only setting us on our feet because we are already upside down, with our nose to the ground and our feet kicking against the heavens. I just plagiarized one of his images there; it is impossible not to. Someone said that GKC's sayings are like potato chips: it's impossible to eat just one. They are gloriously addictive.

GKC is a gold mine, and here are some gold potato chips.

Peter Kreeft

Publisher's Note

The sources for each of the following twenty-six chapters are listed on pages 179–180, revealing the Chesterton book and chapter from which that selection is taken.

Occasionally, you will see brief notes in brackets [ ]. We have kept these to a minimum, but every now and then we believed that a word or phrase or reference needed some explanation for the sake of twenty-first century readers.

British English spellings have been changed to American English versions, for instance, "sceptical" to "skeptical," "colour" to "color," and "to-day" to "today."

A couple of words have also been changed, not for their spelling but for their rendering. Among these, we've changed "Mahomet" to "Muhammed." We'd be remiss if we didn't acknowledge that Chesterton himself predicted this day would come—and, to character, grumbled about it. He wrote: "I am . . . aware that some are sensitive about the spelling of words; and the very proof-readers will sometimes revolt and turn Mahomet into Mohammed. Upon this point, however, I am unrepentant; for I never could see the point of altering a form with historic and even heroic fame in our own language, for the sake of reproducing by an arrangement of our letters something that is really written in quite different letters, and probably pronounced with a quite different accent." We very respectfully disagree.

A

Asceticism

If ever that rarer sort of romantic love, which was the truth that sustained the Troubadours, falls out of fashion and is treated as fiction, we may see some such misunderstanding as that of the modern world about asceticism. For it seems conceivable that some barbarians might try to destroy chivalry in love, as the barbarians ruling in Berlin destroyed chivalry in war. [World War I had just ended.] If that were ever so, we should have the same sort of unintelligent sneers and unimaginative questions. Men will ask what selfish sort of woman it must have been who ruthlessly exacted tribute in the form of flowers, or what an avaricious creature she can have been to demand solid gold in the form of a ring; just as they ask what cruel kind of God can have demanded sacrifice and self-denial. They will have lost the clue to all that lovers have meant by love; and will not understand that it was because the thing was not demanded that it was done. But whether or not any such lesser things will throw a light on the greater, it is utterly useless to study a great thing like the Franciscan movement while remaining in the modern mood that murmurs against gloomy asceticism. The whole point about St. Francis of Assisi is that he certainly was ascetical and he certainly was not gloomy. As soon as ever he had been unhorsed by the glorious humiliation of his vision of dependence on the divine love, he flung himself into fasting and vigil exactly as he had flung himself furiously into battle. He had wheeled his charger clean round, but there was no halt or check in the thundering impetuosity of his charge. There was nothing negative about it; it was not a regimen or a stoical simplicity of life. It was not self-denial merely in the sense of self-control. It was as positive as a passion; it had all the air of being as positive as a pleasure. He devoured fasting as a man devours food. He plunged after poverty as men have dug madly for gold. And it is precisely the positive and passionate quality of this part of his personality that is a challenge to the modern mind in the whole problem of the pursuit of pleasure. There undeniably is the historical fact; and there attached to it is another moral fact almost as undeniable. It is certain that he held on this heroic or unnatural course from the moment when he went forth in his hair-shirt into the winter woods to the moment when he desired even in his death agony to lie bare upon the bare ground, to prove that he had and that he was nothing. And we can say, with almost as deep a certainty, that the stars which passed above that gaunt and wasted corpse stark upon the rocky floor had for once, in all their shining cycles round the world of laboring humanity, looked down upon a happy man.

B

Bethlehem

This sketch of the human story began in a cave; the cave which popular science associates with the cave-man and in which practical discovery has really found archaic drawings of animals. The second half of human history, which was like a new creation of the world, also begins in a cave. There is even a shadow of such a fancy in the fact that animals were again present; for it was a cave used as a stable by the mountaineers of the uplands about Bethlehem; who still drive their cattle into such holes and caverns at night. It was here that a homeless couple had crept underground with the cattle when the doors of the crowded caravanserai had been shut in their faces; and it was here beneath the very feet of the passers-by, in a cellar under the very floor of the world, that Jesus Christ was born. But in that second creation there was indeed something symbolical in the roots of the primeval rock or the horns of the prehistoric herd. God also was a Cave-Man, and had also traced strange shapes of creatures, curiously colored, upon the wall of the world; but the pictures that he made had come to life.

A mass of legend and literature, which increases and will never end, has repeated and rung the changes on that single paradox; that the hands that had made the sun and stars were too small to reach the huge heads of the cattle. Upon this paradox, we might almost say upon this jest, all the literature of our faith is founded. It is at least like a jest in this, that it is something which the scientific critic cannot see. He laboriously explains the difficulty which we have always defiantly and almost derisively exaggerated; and mildly condemns as improbable something that we have almost madly exalted as incredible; as something that would be much too good to be true, except that it is true. When that contrast between the cosmic creation and the little local infancy has been repeated, reiterated, underlined, emphasized, exulted in, sung, shouted, roared, not to say howled, in a hundred thousand hymns, carols, rhymes, rituals, pictures, poems, and popular sermons, it may be suggested that we hardly need a higher critic to draw our attention to something a little odd about it; especially one of the sort that seems to take a long time to see a joke, even his own joke. But about this contrast and combination of ideas one thing may be said here, because it is relevant to the whole thesis of this book. The sort of modern critic of whom I speak is generally much impressed with the importance of education in life and the importance of psychology in education. That sort of man is never tired of telling us that first impressions fix character by the law of causation; and he will become quite nervous if a child's visual sense is poisoned by the wrong colors on a golliwog or his nervous system prematurely shaken by a cacophonous rattle. Yet he will think us very narrow-minded, if we say that this is exactly why there really is a difference between being brought up as a Christian and being brought up as a Jew or a Muslim or an atheist. The difference is that every Catholic child has learned from pictures, and even every Protestant child from stories, this incredible combination of contrasted ideas as one of the very first impressions on his mind. It is not merely a theological difference. It is a psychological difference which can outlast any theologies. It really is, as that sort of scientist loves to say about anything, incurable. Any agnostic or atheist whose childhood has known a real Christmas has ever afterwards, whether he likes it or not, an association in his mind between two ideas that most of mankind must regard as remote from each other; the idea of a baby and the idea of unknown strength that sustains the stars. His instincts and imagination can still connect them, when his reason can no longer see the need of the connection; for him there will always be some savor of religion about the mere picture of a mother and a baby; some hint of mercy and softening about the mere mention of the dreadful name of God. But the two ideas are not naturally or necessarily combined. They would not be necessarily combined for an ancient Greek . . . even for Aristotle. It is no more inevitable to connect God with an infant than to connect gravitation with a kitten. It has been created in our minds by Christmas because we are Christians, because we are psychological Christians even when we are not theological ones. In other words, this combination of ideas has emphatically, in the much disputed phrase, altered human nature. There is really a difference between the man who knows it and the man who does not. It may not be a difference of moral worth, for the Muslim or the Jew might be worthier according to his lights; but it is a plain fact about the crossing of two particular lights, the conjunction of two stars in our particular horoscope. Omnipotence and impotence, or divinity and infancy, do definitely make a sort of epigram which a million repetitions cannot turn into a platitude. It is not unreasonable to call it unique. Bethlehem is emphatically a place where extremes meet.

Here begins, it is needless to say, another mighty influence for the humanization of Christendom. If the world wanted what is called a non-controversial aspect of Christianity, it would probably select Christmas. Yet it is obviously bound up with what is supposed to be a controversial aspect (I could never at any stage of my opinions imagine why); the respect paid to the Blessed Virgin. When I was a boy a more Puritan generation objected to a statue upon my parish church representing the Virgin and Child. After much controversy, they compromised by taking away the Child. One would think that this was even more corrupted with Mariolatry, unless the mother was counted less dangerous when deprived of a sort of weapon. But the practical difficulty is also a parable. You cannot chip away the statue of a mother from all round that of a new-born child. You cannot suspend the newborn child in mid-air; indeed you cannot really have a statue of a newborn child at all. Similarly, you cannot suspend the idea of a newborn child in the void or think of him without thinking of his mother. You cannot visit the child without visiting the mother; you cannot in common human life approach the child except through the mother. If we are to think of Christ in this aspect at all, the other idea follows as it is followed in history. We must either leave Christ out of Christmas, or Christmas out of Christ, or we must admit, if only as we admit it in an old picture, that those holy heads are too near together for the haloes not to mingle and cross.

C

Catholicism

The first fallacy about the Catholic Church is the idea
that it is a church. I mean that it is a church in the sense
in which the Nonconformist [a Protestant dissenter
from the Church of England] newspapers talk about
The Churches. I do not intend any expression of contempt about The Churches; nor is it an expression of
contempt to say that it would be more convenient to
call them the sects. This is true in a much deeper and
more sympathetic sense than may at first appear; but
to begin with, it is certainly true in a perfectly plain
and historical sense, which has nothing to do with
sympathy at all. Thus, for instance, I have much more
sympathy for small nationalities than I have for small
sects. But it is simply a historical fact that the Roman
Empire was the Empire and that it was not a small
nationality. And it is simply a historical fact that the
Roman Church is the Church and is not a sect. Nor
is there anything narrow or unreasonable in saying
that the Church is the Church. It may be a good thing
that the Roman Empire broke up into nations; but it
certainly was not one of the nations into which it broke
up. And even a person who thinks it fortunate that
the Church broke up into sects ought to be able to distinguish between the little things he likes and the big

thing he has broken. As a matter of fact, in the case of things so large, so unique and so creative of the culture about them as were the Roman Empire and the Roman Church, it is not controversial but simply correct to confine the one word to the one example.

Everybody who originally used the word "Empire" used it of that Empire; everybody who used the word "Ecclesia" used it of that Ecclesia. There may have been similar things in other places, but they could not be called by the same name for the simple reason that they were not named in the same language. We know what we mean by a Roman Emperor; we can if we like talk of a Chinese Emperor, just as we can if we like take a particular sort of a Mandarin and say he is equivalent to a Marquis. But we never can be certain that he is exactly equivalent; for the thing we are thinking about is peculiar to our own history and in that sense stands alone. Now in that, if in no other sense, the Catholic Church stands alone. It does not merely belong to a class of Christian churches. It does not merely belong to a class of human religions. Considered quite coldly and impartially, as by a man from the moon, it is much more *sui generis* [Latin, "in a class by itself"] than that. It is, if the critic chooses to think so, the ruin of an attempt at a Universal Religion which was bound to fail. But calling the wreckers to break up a ship does not turn the ship into one of its own timbers; and cutting Poland up into three pieces does not make Poland the same as Posen [a West Prussian province created by the German Weimar Republic].

But in a much more profound and philosophical sense this notion that the Church is one of the sects is the great fallacy of the whole affair. It is a matter more psychological and more difficult to describe. But it is perhaps the most sensational of the silent upheavals or reversals in the mind that constitute the revolution called conversion. Every man conceives himself as moving about in a cosmos of some kind; and the man of the days of my youth walked about in a kind of vast and airy Crystal Palace in which there were exhibits set side by side. The cosmos, being made of glass and iron, was partly transparent and partly colorless; anyhow, there was something negative about it; arching over all our heads, a roof as remote as a sky, it seemed to be impartial and impersonal. Our attention was fixed on the exhibits, which were all carefully ticketed and arranged in rows; for it was the age of science. Here stood all the religions in a row—the churches or sects or whatever we called them; and towards the end of the row there was a particularly dingy and dismal one, with a pointed roof half fallen in and pointed windows most broken with stones by passers-by; and we were told that this particular exhibit was the Roman Catholic Church. Some of us were sorry for it and even fancied it had been rather badly used; most of us regarded it as dirty and disreputable; a few of us even pointed out that many details in the ruin were artistically beautiful or architecturally important. But most people preferred to deal at other and more business-like booths; at the Quaker shop of Peace and Plenty or the Salvation Army store where the showman beats the big drum outside. Now conversion consists very largely, on its intellectual side, in the discovery that all that picture of equal creeds inside an indifferent cosmos is quite false. It is not a question of comparing the merits and defects of the Quaker meeting-house set beside the Catholic cathedral. It is the Quaker meeting-house that is inside the Catholic cathedral; it is the Catholic

cathedral that covers everything like the vault of the
Crystal Palace; and it is when we look up at the vast
distant dome covering all the exhibits that we trace
the Gothic roof and the pointed windows. In other
words, Quakerism is but a temporary form of Quietism
which has arisen technically outside the Church as the
Quietism of Fenelon appeared technically inside the
Church. But both were in themselves temporary and
would have, like Fenelon [François Fénelon, 1651–1715,
French archbishop who was once caught up in a Quiet-
ist controversy], sooner or later to return to the Church
in order to live. The principle of life in all these varia-
tions of Protestantism, in so far as it is not a principle
of death, consists of what remained in them of Catholic Christendom; and to Catholic Christendom they
have always returned to be recharged with vitality. I
know that this will sound like a statement to be chal-
lenged; but it is true. The return of Catholic ideas to
the separated parts of Christendom was often indeed
indirect. But though the influence came through many,
centrist it always came from one. It came through the
Romantic Movement, a glimpse of the mere picturesqueness of medievalism; but it is something more
than an accident that Romances, like Romance languages, are named after Rome. . . . Or it came from the
Pre-Raphaelites or the opening of continental art and
culture by Matthew Arnold and Morris and Ruskin
and the rest [nineteenth-century writers and artists].
But examine the actual make-up of the mind of a good
Quaker or Congregational minister at this moment,
and compare it with the mind of such a dissenter in the
Little Bethel before such culture came. And you will
see how much of his health and happiness he owes to
Ruskin and what Ruskin owed to Giotto; to Morris and

what Morris owed to Chaucer; to fine scholars of his own school like Philip Wicksteed [translator of Dante], and what they owe to Dante and St. Thomas. Such a man will still sometimes talk of the Middle Ages as the Dark Ages. But the Dark Ages have improved the wallpaper on his wall and the dress on his wife and all the whole dingy and vulgar life which he live[s]. . . . For he also is a Christian and lives only by the life of Christendom.

It is not easy to express this enormous inversion which I have here tried to suggest in the image of a world turned inside out. I mean that the thing which had been stared at as a small something swells out and swallows everything. Christendom is in the literal sense a continent. We come to feel that it contains everything, even the things in revolt against itself. But it is perhaps the most towering intellectual transformation of all and the one that it is hardest to undo even for the sake of argument. It is almost impossible even in imagination to reverse that reversal. Another way of putting it is to say that we have come to regard all these historical figures as characters in Catholic history, even if they are not Catholics. And in a certain sense, the historical as distinct from the theological sense, they never do cease to be Catholic. They are not people who have really created something entirely new, until they actually pass the border of reason and create more or less crazy nightmares. But nightmares do not last; and most of them even now are in various stages of waking up. Protestants are Catholics gone wrong; that is what is really meant by saying they are Christians. Sometimes they have gone very wrong; but not often have they gone right ahead with their own particular wrong. Thus a Calvinist is a Catholic obsessed with the Catholic idea of the sovereignty of God. But when he makes it mean that God wishes particular people to be damned, we may say with all restraint that he has become a rather morbid Catholic. In point of fact he is a diseased Catholic; and the disease left to itself would be death or madness. But, as a matter of fact, the disease did not last long, and is itself now practically dead. But every step he takes back towards humanity is a step back towards Catholicism. Thus a Quaker is a, Catholic obsessed with the Catholic idea of gentle simplicity and truth. But when he made it mean that it is a lie to say "you" and an act of idolatry to take off your hat to a lady, it is not too much to say that whether or not he had a hat off, he certainly had a tile loose. But as a matter of fact he himself found it necessary to dispense with the eccentricity (and the hat) and to leave the straight road that would have led him to a lunatic asylum. Only every step he takes back towards common sense is a step back towards Catholicism. In so far as he was right he was a Catholic; and in so far as he was wrong he has not himself been able to remain a Protestant.

. . . In short, the story of these sects is not one of straight lines striking outwards and onwards, though if it were they would all be striking in different directions. It is a pattern of curves continually returning into the continent and common life of their and our civilization; and the summary of that civilization and central sanity is the philosophy of the Catholic Church . . .

When the convert has once seen the world . . . with one balance of ideas and a number of other ideas that have left it and lost their balance, he does not in fact experience any of the inconveniences that he might reasonably have feared before that silent but stunning revolution. He is not worried by being told that there is something in Spiritualism or something in Christian Science. He knows there is something in everything. But he is moved by the more impressive fact that he finds everything in something. And he is quite sure that if these investigators really are looking for everything, and not merely looking for anything, they will be more and more likely to look for it in the same place. In that sense he is far less worried about them than he was when he thought that one or other of them might be the only person having any sort of communication with the higher mysteries and obviously rather capable of making a mess of it. He is no more likely to be overawed by the fact that Mrs. Eddy [Mary Baker Eddy, founder of Christian Science] achieved spiritual healing or Mr. Home achieved bodily levitation than a fully dressed gentleman in Bond Street would be overawed by the top-hat on the head of a naked savage. A top-hat may be a good hat but it is a bad costume. And a magnetic trick may be a sufficient sensation but it is a very insufficient philosophy. He is no more envious of a Bolshevist for making a revolution than of a beaver for making a dam; for he knows his own civilization can make things on a pattern not quite so simple or so monotonous. But he believes this of his civilization and his religion and not merely of himself. There is nothing supercilious about his attitude; because he is well aware that he has only scratched the surface of the spiritual estate that is now open to him. In other words, the convert does not in the least abandon investigation or even adventure. He does not think he knows everything, nor has he lost curiosity about the things he does not know. But experience has taught him that he will find nearly everything somewhere inside that estate

and that a very large number of people are finding
next to nothing outside it. For the estate is not only a
formal garden or an ordered farm; there is plenty of
hunting and fishing on it, and, as the phrase goes, very
good sport.

For this is one of the very queerest of the common delusions about what happens to the convert. In
some muddled way people have confused the natural
remarks of converts, about having found moral peace,
with some idea of their having found mental rest, in
the sense of mental inaction. They might as well say
that a man who has completely recovered his health,
after an attack of palsy or St. Vitus' dance, signalizes
his healthy state by sitting absolutely still like a stone.
Recovering his health means recovering his power of
moving in the right way as distinct from the wrong
way; but he will probably move a great deal more than
before. To become a Catholic is not to leave off thinking, but to learn how to think. It is so in exactly the
same sense in which to recover from palsy is not to
leave off moving but to learn how to move. The Catholic convert has for the first time a starting-point for
straight and strenuous thinking. He has for the first
time a way of testing the truth in any question that
he raises. As the world goes, especially at present, it
is the other people, the heathen and the heretics, who
seem to have every virtue except the power of connected thought. There was indeed a brief period when
a small minority did some hard thinking on the heathen or heretical side. It barely lasted from the time of
Voltaire to the time of Huxley [Thomas Huxley, early
prominent advocate of Darwin's theory of evolution].
It has now entirely disappeared. What is now called
free thought is valued, not because it is free thought,

but because it is freedom from thought; because it is free thoughtlessness.

Nothing is more amusing to the convert, when his conversion has been complete for some time, than to hear the speculations about when or whether he will repent of the conversion; when he will be sick of it, how long he will stand it, at what stage of his external exasperation he will start up and say he can bear it no more. For all this is founded on that optical illusion about the outside and the inside which I have tried to sketch in this chapter. The outsiders, stand by and see, or think they see, the convert entering with bowed head a sort of small temple which they are convinced is fitted up inside like a prison, if not a torture-chamber. But all they really know about it is that he has passed through a door. They do not know that he has not gone into the inner darkness, but out into the broad daylight. It is he who is, in the beautiful and beatific sense of the word, an outsider. He does not want to go into a larger room, because he does not know of any larger room to go into. He knows of a large number of much smaller rooms, each of which is labelled as being very large; but he is quite sure he would be cramped in any of them. . . .

But each of these cosmic systems or machines seems to him much smaller and even much simpler than the broad and balanced universe in which he lives. One of them is labelled Agnostic; but he knows by experience that it has not really even the freedom of ignorance. It is a wheel that must always go round without a single jolt of miraculous interruption—a circle that must not be squared by any higher mathematics of mysticism; a machine that must be scoured as clean of all spirits as if it were the avowed machine of materialism. In living in a world with two orders, the supernatural and the natural, the convert feels he is living in a larger world and does not feel any temptation to crawl back into a smaller one. One of them is labelled Theosophical or Buddhist; but he knows by experience that it is only the same sort of wearisome wheel used for spiritual things instead of material things. Living in a world where he is free to do anything, even to go to the devil, he does not see why he should tie himself to the wheel of a mere destiny. One of them is labelled Humanitarian; but he knows that such humanitarians have really far less experience of humanity. He knows that they are thinking almost entirely of men as they are at this moment in modern cities, and have nothing like the huge human interest of what began by being preached to legionaries in Palestine and is still being preached to peasants in China. So clear is this perception that I have sometimes put it to myself, as something between a melancholy meditation and a joke. "Where should I go now, if I did leave the Catholic Church?" I certainly would not go to any of those little social sects which only express one idea at a time, because that idea happens to be fashionable at the moment. The best I could hope for would be to wander away into the woods and become, not a Pantheist (for that is also a limitation and a bore) but rather a pagan, in the mood to cry out that some particular mountain peak or flowering fruit tree was sacred and a thing to be worshipped. That at least would be beginning all over again; but it would bring me back to the same problem in the end. If it was reasonable to have a sacred tree it was not unreasonable to have a sacred crucifix; and if the god was to be found on one peak he may as reasonably be found under one spire. To find a new religion is sooner or later to have found one; and why should I have been discontented with the one I had found? Especially, as I said in the first words of this essay, when it is the one old religion which seems capable of remaining new.

I know very well that if I went upon that journey I should either despair or return; and that none of the trees would ever be a substitute for the real sacred tree. Paganism is better than pantheism, for paganism is free to imagine divinities, while pantheism is forced to pretend, in a priggish way, that all things are equally divine. But I should not imagine any divinity that was sufficiently divine. I seem to know that weary return through the woodlands; for I think in some symbolic fashion I have walked that road before. For as I have tried to confess here without excessive egotism, I think I am the sort of man who came to Christ from Pan and Dionysus and not from Luther or Laud; that the conversion I understand is that of the pagan and not the Puritan; and upon that antique conversion is founded the whole world that we know. It is a transformation far more vast and tremendous than anything that has been meant for many years past, at least in England and America, by a sectarian controversy or a doctrinal division. On the height of that ancient empire and that international experience, humanity had a vision. It has not had another; but only quarrels about that one. Paganism was the largest thing in the world and Christianity was larger; and everything else has been comparatively small.

D

Charles Dickens

Jesus Christ was destined to found a faith which made the rich poorer and the poor rich; but even when He was going to enrich them, He began with the phrase, "Blessed are the poor." The Gissings and the Gorkys [novelists George Gissing and Maxim Gorky] say, as a universal literary motto, "Cursed are the poor." Among a million who have faintly followed Christ in this divine contradiction, Dickens stands out especially. He said, in all his reforming utterances, "Cure poverty"; but he said in all his actual descriptions, "Blessed are the poor." He described their happiness, and men rushed to remove their sorrow. He described them as human, and men resented the insults to their humanity. It is not difficult to see why . . . Dickens's denunciations have had so much more practical an effect than the denunciations of such a man as Gissing. Both agreed that the souls of the people were in a kind of prison. But Gissing said that the prison was full of dead souls. Dickens said that the prison was full of living souls. And the fiery cavalcade of rescuers felt that they had not come too late.

Of this general fact about Dickens's descriptions of poverty there will not, I suppose, be any serious dispute. . . . No one will deny that he made a special

feature of the poor. . . . It is here sufficient to regis-
ter in conclusion of our examination of the reforming
optimist, that Dickens certainly was such an optimist,
and that he made it his business to insist upon what
happiness there is in the lives of the unhappy. His poor
man is always . . . a man the optimism of whose spirit
increases if anything with the pessimism of his experience. It can also be registered as a fact equally solid
and quite equally demonstrable that this optimistic
Dickens did affect great reforms.

The reforms in which Dickens was instrumental
were indeed, from the point of view of our sweeping
social panaceas, special and limited. But perhaps, for
that reason especially, they afford a compact and concrete instance of the psychological paradox of which
we speak. Dickens did definitely destroy—or at the
very least help to destroy—certain institutions; he
destroyed those institutions simply by describing
them. But the crux and peculiarity of the whole matter is this, that, in a sense, it can really be said that
he described these things too optimistically. In a real
sense, he described Dotheboys Hall [from *Nicholas
Nickleby*] as a better place than it is. In a real sense, he
made out the workhouse as a pleasanter place than it
can ever be. For the chief glory of Dickens is that he
made these places interesting; and the chief infamy of
England is that it has made these places dull. Dullness
was the thing that Dickens's genius could never succeed in describing; his vitality was so violent that he
could not introduce into his books the genuine impression even of a moment of monotony. If there is anywhere in his novels an instant of silence, we only hear
more clearly the hero whispering with the heroine, the
villain sharpening his dagger, or the creaking of the

machinery that is to give out the god from the machine. He could splendidly describe gloomy places, but he could not describe dreary places. He could describe miserable marriages, but not monotonous marriages. It must have been genuinely entertaining to be married to Mr. Quilp [from *The Old Curiosity Shop*]. This sense of a still incessant excitement he spreads over every inch of his story, and over every dark tract of his landscape. His idea of a desolate place is a place where anything can happen, he has no idea of that desolate place where nothing can happen. This is a good thing for his soul, for the place where nothing can happen is hell. But still, it might reasonably be maintained by the modern mind that he is hampered in describing human evil and sorrow by this inability to imagine tedium, this dullness in the matter of dullness. For, after all, it is certainly true that the worst part of the lot of the unfortunate is the fact that they have long spaces in which to review the irrevocability of their doom. It is certainly true that the worst days of the oppressed man are the nine days out of ten in which he is not oppressed. This sense of sickness and sameness Dickens did certainly fail or refuse to give. . . . He made out the bad school, the bad parochial system, the bad debtor's prison as very much jollier and more exciting than they may really have been. In a sense, then, he flattered them; but he destroyed them with the flattery. By making Mrs. Gamp [from *Martin Chuzzlewit*] delightful he made her impossible. He gave every one an interest in Mr. Bumble's [from *Oliver Twist*] existence; and by the same act gave every one an interest in his destruction. It would be difficult to find a stronger instance of the utility and energy of the method which we have, for the sake of argument, called the method of the optimistic reformer.

As long as low Yorkshire schools were entirely colorless and dreary, they continued quietly tolerated by the public and quietly intolerable to the victims. So long as Squeers [from *Nicholas Nickleby*] was dull as well as cruel he was permitted; the moment he became amusing as well as cruel he was destroyed. As long as Bumble was merely inhuman he was allowed. When he became human, humanity wiped him right out. For in order to do these great acts of justice we must always realize not only the humanity of the oppressed, but even the humanity of the oppressor. The satirist had, in a sense, to create the images in the mind before, as an iconoclast, he could destroy them. Dickens had to make Squeers live before he could make him die.

In connection with the accusation of vulgar optimism . . . there is another somewhat odd thing to notice. Nobody in the world was ever less optimistic than Dickens in his treatment of evil or the evil man. When I say optimist in this matter I mean optimism, in the modern sense, of an attempt to whitewash evil. Nobody ever made less attempt to whitewash evil than Dickens. Nobody black was ever less white than Dickens's black. He painted his villains and lost characters more black than they really are. He crowds his stories with a kind of villain rare in modern fiction—the villain really without any "redeeming point." There is no redeeming point in Squeers, or in Monks, or in Ralph Nickleby, or in Bill Sikes, or in Quilp, or in Brass, or in Mr. Chester, or in Mr. Pecksniff, or in Jonas Chuzzlewit, or in Carker, or in Uriah Heep, or in Blandois, or in a hundred more . . .

Some will dismiss this lurid villainy as a detail of his artificial romance. I am not inclined to do so. He inherited, undoubtedly, this unqualified villain as he inherited so many other things, from the whole history of European literature. But he breathed into the black-guard a peculiar and vigorous life of his own. He did not show any tendency to modify his black-guardism in accordance with the increasing considerateness of the age; he did not seem to wish to make his villain less villainous; he did not wish to imitate the analysis of George Eliot, or the reverent skepticism of Thackeray. And all this works back, I think, to a real thing in him, that he wished to have an obstreperous and incalculable enemy. He wished to keep alive the idea of combat, which means, of necessity, a combat against something individual and alive. I do not know whether, in the kindly rationalism of his epoch, he kept any belief in a personal devil in his theology, but he certainly created a personal devil in every one of his books.

A good example of my meaning can be found, for instance, in such a character as Quilp. Dickens may, for all I know, have had originally some idea of describing Quilp as the bitter and unhappy cripple, a deformity whose mind is stunted along with his body. But if he had such an idea, he soon abandoned it. Quilp is not in the least unhappy. His whole picturesqueness consists in the fact that he has a kind of hellish happiness, an atrocious hilarity that makes him go bounding about like an India rubber ball. Quilp is not in the least bitter; he has an unaffected gaiety, an expansiveness, a universality. He desires to hurt people in the same hearty way that a good-natured man desires to help them. He likes to poison people with the same kind of clamorous camaraderie with which an honest man likes to stand them drink. Quilp is not in the least stunted in mind; he is not in reality even stunted in body—his body, that is, does not in any way fall short of what he wants it to do. His smallness gives him rather the promptitude of a bird or the precipitance of a bullet. In a word, Quilp is precisely the devil of the Middle Ages; he belongs to that amazingly healthy period when even lost spirits were hilarious.

This heartiness and vivacity in the villains of Dickens is worthy of note because it is directly connected with his own cheerfulness. This is a truth little understood in our time, but it is a very essential one. If optimism means a general approval, it is certainly true that the more a man becomes an optimist the more he becomes a melancholy man. If he manages to praise everything, his praise will develop an alarming resemblance to a polite boredom. He will say that the marsh is as good as the garden; he will mean that the garden is as dull as the marsh. He may force himself to say that emptiness is good, but he will hardly prevent himself from asking what is the good of such good. This optimism does exist—this optimism which is more hopeless than pessimism—this optimism which is the very heart of hell.

Against such an aching vacuum of joyless approval there is only one antidote—a sudden and pugnacious belief in positive evil. This world can be made beautiful again by beholding it as a battlefield. When we have defined and isolated the evil thing, the colors come back into everything else. When evil things have become evil, good things, in a blazing apocalypse, become good. There are some men who are dreary because they do not believe in God; but there are many others who are dreary because they do not believe in the devil. The grass grows green again when we believe in the devil, the roses grow red again when we believe in the devil.

No man was more filled with the sense of this bellicose basis of all cheerfulness than Dickens. He knew very well the essential truth, that the true optimist can only continue an optimist so long as he is discontented. For the full value of this life can only be got by fighting; the violent take it by storm. And if we have accepted everything, we have missed something—war. This life of ours is a very enjoyable fight, but a very miserable truce. And it appears strange to me that so few critics of Dickens or of other romantic writers have noticed this philosophical meaning in the undiluted villain. The villain is not in the story to be a character; he is there to be a danger—a ceaseless, ruthless, and uncompromising menace, like that of wild beasts or the sea. For the full satisfaction of the sense of combat, which everywhere and always involves a sense of equality, it is necessary to make the evil thing a man; but it is not always necessary, it is not even always artistic, to make him a mixed and probable man. In any tale, the tone of which is at all symbolic, he may quite legitimately be made an aboriginal and infernal energy. He must be a man only in the sense that he must have a wit and will to be matched with the wit and will of the man chiefly fighting. The evil may be inhuman, but it must not be impersonal, which is almost exactly the position occupied by Satan in the theological scheme.

But when all is said . . . the chief fountain in Dickens of what I have called cheerfulness, and some prefer to call optimism, is something deeper than a verbal philosophy. It is, after all, an incomparable hunger and pleasure for the vitality and the variety, for the infinite eccentricity of existence. And this word "eccentricity" brings us, perhaps, nearer to the matter than any other. It is, perhaps, the strongest mark of the divinity of man

that he talks of this world as "a strange world," though
he has seen no other. We feel that all there is eccentric,
though we do not know what is the center. This sentiment of the grotesqueness of the universe ran through
Dickens's brain and body like the mad blood of the
elves. He saw all his streets in fantastic perspectives,
he saw all his cockney villas as top heavy and wild,
he saw every man's nose twice as big as it was, and
very man's eyes like saucers. And this was the basis
of his gaiety—the only real basis of any philosophical
gaiety. This world is not to be justified as it is justified
by the mechanical optimists; it is not to be justified as
the best of all possible worlds. Its merit is not that it is
orderly and explicable; its merit is that it is wild and
utterly unexplained. Its merit is precisely that none of
us could have conceived such a thing, that we should
have rejected the bare idea of it as miracle and unreason. It is the best of all impossible worlds.

E

Ephemera

I cannot understand the people who take literature
seriously; but I can love them, and I do. Out of my love
I warn them to keep clear of this book. It is a collection
of crude and shapeless papers upon current or rather
flying subjects. . . . They were written, as a rule, at the
last moment; they were handed in the moment before
it was too late, and I do not think that our common-
wealth would have been shaken to its foundations if
they had been handed in the moment after. They must
go out now, with all their imperfections on their head,
or rather on mine; for their vices are too vital to be
improved with a blue pencil, or with anything I can
think of, except dynamite.

Their chief vice is that so many of them are very
serious; because I had no time to make them flippant.
It is so easy to be solemn; it is so hard to be frivolous.
Let any honest reader shut his eyes for a few moments,
and approaching the secret tribunal of his soul, ask
himself whether he would really rather be asked in
the next two hours to write the front page of the *Times*,
which is full of long leading articles, or the front page
of *Tit-Bits*, which is full of short jokes. If the reader
is the fine conscientious fellow I take him for, he will
at once reply that he would rather on the spur of the

moment write ten *Times* articles than one *Tit-Bits* joke. Responsibility, a heavy and cautious responsibility of speech, is the easiest thing in the world; anybody can do it. That is why so many tired, elderly, and wealthy men go in for politics. They are responsible, because they have not the strength of mind left to be irresponsible. It is more dignified to sit still than to dance the Barn Dance. It is also easier. So in these easy pages I keep myself on the whole on the level of the *Times*: it is only occasionally that I leap upwards almost to the level of *Tit-Bits*.

I resume the defense of this indefensible book. These articles have another disadvantage arising from the scurry in which they were written; they are too long-winded and elaborate. One of the great disadvantages of hurry is that it takes such a long time. If I have to start for High-gate this day, I may perhaps go the shortest way. If I have to start this minute, I shall almost certainly go the longest. In these essays (as I read them over) I feel frightfully annoyed with myself for not getting to the point more quickly; but I had not enough leisure to be quick. There are several maddening cases in which I took two or three pages in attempting to describe an attitude of which the essence could be expressed in an epigram; only there was no time for epigrams. I do not repent of one shade of opinion here expressed; but I feel that they might have been expressed so much more briefly and precisely. For instance, these pages contain a sort of recurring protest against the boast of certain writers that they are merely recent. They brag that their philosophy of the universe is the last philosophy or the new philosophy, or the advanced and progressive philosophy. I have said much against a mere modernism.

When I use the word "modernism," I am not alluding specially to the current quarrel in the Roman Catholic Church, though I am certainly astonished at any intellectual group accepting so weak and unphilosophical a name. It is incomprehensible to me that any thinker can calmly call himself a modernist; he might as well call himself a Thursdayite. But apart altogether from that particular disturbance, I am conscious of a general irritation expressed against the people who boast of their advancement and modernity in the discussion of religion. But I never succeeded in saying the quite clear and obvious thing that is really the matter with modernism. The real objection to modernism is simply that it is a form of snobbishness. It is an attempt to crush a rational opponent not by reason, but by some mystery of superiority, by hinting that one is especially up to date or particularly "in the know." To flaunt the fact that we have had all the last books from Germany is simply vulgar; like flaunting the fact that we have had all the last bonnets from Paris. To introduce into philosophical discussions a sneer at a creed's antiquity is like introducing a sneer at a lady's age. It is caddish because it is irrelevant. The pure modernist is merely a snob; he cannot bear to be a month behind the fashion.

Similarly I find that I have tried in these pages to express the real objection to philanthropists and have not succeeded. I have not seen the quite simple objection to the causes advocated by certain wealthy idealists; causes of which the cause called teetotalism is the strongest case. I have used many abusive terms about the thing, calling it Puritanism, or superciliousness, or aristocracy; but I have not seen and stated the quite simple objection to philanthropy, which is that it is religious persecution. Religious persecution does not consist in thumbscrews or fires of Smithfield [area of London where heretics were executed]; the essence of religious persecution is this: that the man who happens to have material power in the State, either by wealth or by official position, should govern his fellow-citizens not according to their religion or philosophy, but according to his own. If, for instance, there is such a thing as a vegetarian nation; if there is a great united mass of men who wish to live by the vegetarian morality, then I say in the emphatic words of the arrogant French marquis before the French Revolution, "Let them eat grass." Perhaps that French oligarch was a humanitarian; most oligarchs are. Perhaps when he told the peasants to eat grass he was recommending to them the hygienic simplicity of a vegetarian restaurant. But that is an irrelevant, though most fascinating, speculation. The point here is that if a nation is really vegetarian let its government force upon it the whole horrible weight of vegetarianism. Let its government give the national guests a State vegetarian banquet. Let its government, in the most literal and awful sense of the words, give them beans. That sort of tyranny is all very well; for it is the people tyrannizing over all the persons. But "temperance reformers" are like a small group of vegetarians who should silently and systematically act on an ethical assumption entirely unfamiliar to the mass of the people. They would always be giving peerages to greengrocers. They would always be appointing Parliamentary Commissions to enquire into the private life of butchers. Whenever they found a man quite at their mercy, as a pauper or a convict or a lunatic, they would force him to add the final touch to his inhuman isolation by becoming a vegetarian. All the meals for school children will be vegetarian meals.

All the State public houses will be vegetarian public houses. There is a very strong case for vegetarianism as compared with teetotalism. Drinking one glass of beer cannot by any philosophy be drunkenness; but killing one animal can, by this philosophy, be murder. The objection to both processes is not that the two creeds, teetotal and vegetarian, are not admissible; it is simply that they are not admitted. The thing is religious persecution because it is not based on the existing religion of the democracy. These people ask the poor to accept in practice what they know perfectly well that the poor would not accept in theory. That is the very definition of religious persecution. I was against the Tory attempt to force upon ordinary Englishmen a Catholic theology in which they do not believe. I am even more against the attempt to force upon them a Muslim morality which they actively deny.

. . . The last indictment against this book is the worst of all. It is simply this: that if all goes well this book will be unintelligible gibberish. For it is mostly concerned with attacking attitudes which are in their nature accidental and incapable of enduring. Brief as is the career of such a book as this, it may last just twenty minutes longer than most of the philosophies that it attacks. In the end it will not matter to us whether we wrote well or ill; whether we fought with flails or reeds. It will matter to us greatly on what side we fought.

F

St. Francis

No man who has been given the freedom of the Faith is likely to fall into those hole–and–corner extravagances in which later degenerate Franciscans, or rather Fraticelli [extreme proponents of poverty, inspired by Francis's Rule, eventually declared heretical], sought to concentrate entirely on St. Francis as a second Christ, the creator of a new gospel. In fact any such notion makes nonsense of every motive in the man's life; for no man would reverently magnify what he was meant to rival, or only profess to follow what he existed to supplant. On the contrary . . . this little study would rather especially insist that it was really the papal sagacity that saved the great Franciscan movement for the whole world and the universal Church, and prevented it from petering out as that sort of stale and second rate sect that is called a new religion. Everything that is written here must be understood not only as distinct from but diametrically opposed to the idolatry of the Fraticelli. The difference between Christ and St. Francis was the difference between the Creator and the creature; and certainly no creature was ever so conscious of that colossal contrast as St. Francis himself. But subject to this understanding, it is perfectly true and it is vitally important that Christ was the pattern

on which St. Francis sought to fashion himself; and that
at many points their human and historical lives were
even curiously coincident; and above all, that compared to most of us at least St. Francis is a most sublime approximation to his Master, and, even in being
an intermediary and a reflection, is a splendid and yet
a merciful Mirror of Christ. And this truth suggests
another, which I think has hardly been noticed; but
which happens to be a highly forcible argument for the
authority of Christ being continuous in the Catholic
Church.

Cardinal Newman [Blessed John Henry Newman,
English, 1801–1890] wrote in his liveliest controversial
work a sentence that might be a model of what we
mean by saying that his creed tends to lucidity and
logical courage. In speaking of the ease with which
truth may be made to look like its own shadow or
sham, he said, "And if Antichrist is like Christ, Christ
I suppose is like Antichrist." Mere religious sentiment
might well be shocked at the end of the sentence; but
nobody could object to it except the logician who said
that Caesar and Pompey were very much alike, especially Pompey. It may give a much milder shock if I
say here, what most of us have forgotten, that if St.
Francis was like Christ, Christ was to that extent like
St. Francis. And my present point is that it is really very
enlightening to realize that Christ was like St. Francis.
What I mean is this; that if men find certain riddles and
hard sayings in the story of Galilee, and if they find
the answers to those riddles in the story of Assisi, it
really does show that a secret has been handed down
in one religious tradition and no other. It shows that
the casket that was locked in Palestine can be unlocked
in Umbria; for the Church is the keeper of the keys.

Now in truth while it has always seemed natural to explain St. Francis in the light of Christ, it has not occurred to many people to explain Christ in the light of St. Francis. Perhaps the word "light" is not here the proper metaphor; but the same truth is admitted in the accepted metaphor of the mirror. St. Francis is the mirror of Christ rather as the moon is the mirror of the sun. The moon is much smaller than the sun, but it is also much nearer to us; and being less vivid it is more visible. Exactly in the same sense St. Francis is nearer to us, and being a mere man like ourselves is in that sense more imaginable. Being necessarily less of a mystery, he does not, for us, so much open his mouth in mysteries. Yet as a matter of fact, many minor things that seem mysteries in the mouth of Christ would seem merely characteristic paradoxes in the mouth of St. Francis. It seems natural to reread the more remote incidents with the help of the more recent ones. It is a truism to say that Christ lived before Christianity; and it follows that as a historical figure. He is a figure in heathen history. I mean that the medium in which He moved was not the medium of Christendom but of the old pagan empire; and from that alone, not to mention the distance of time, it follows that His circumstances are more alien to us than those of an Italian monk such as we might meet even today. I suppose the most authoritative commentary can hardly be certain of the current or conventional weight of all His words or phrases; of which of them would then have seemed a common allusion and which a strange fancy. This archaic setting has left many of the sayings standing like hieroglyphics and subject to many and peculiar individual interpretations. Yet it is true of almost any of them that if we simply translate them into the Umbrian

dialect of the first Franciscans, they would seem like
any other part of the Franciscans story; doubtless in
one sense fantastic, but quite familiar. All sorts of critical controversies have revolved around the passage
which bids men consider the lilies of the field and copy
them in taking no thought for the morrow. The skeptic
has alternated between telling us to be true Christians
and do it, and explaining that it is impossible to do.
When he is a communist as well as an atheist, he is
generally doubtful whether to blame us for preaching
what is impracticable or for not instantly putting it into
practice. I am not going to discuss here the point of
ethics and economics; I merely remark that even those
who are puzzled at the saying of Christ would hardly
pause in accepting it as a saying of St. Francis. Nobody
would be surprised to find that he had said, "I beseech
you, little brothers, that you be as wise as Brother Daisy
and Brother Dandelion; for never do they lie awake
thinking of tomorrow, yet they have gold crowns like
kings and emperors or like Charlemagne in all his
glory." Even more bitterness and bewilderment has
arisen about the command to turn the other cheek and
to give the coat to the robber who has taken the cloak.
It is widely held to imply the wickedness of war among
nations about which, in itself, not a word seems to have
been said. Taken thus literally and universally, it much
more clearly implies the wickedness of all law and government. Yet there are many prosperous peacemakers
who are much more shocked at the idea of using the
brute force of soldiers against a powerful foreigner
than they are at using the brute force of policemen
against a poor fellow-citizen. Here again I am content
to point out that the paradox becomes perfectly human
and probable if addressed by Francis to Franciscans.

Nobody would be surprised to read that Brother Juniper did then run after the thief that had stolen his hood, beseeching him to take his gown also; for so St. Francis had commanded him. Nobody would be surprised if St. Francis told a young noble, about to be admitted to his company, that so far from pursuing a brigand to recover his shoes, he ought to pursue him to make him a present of his stockings. We may like or not the atmosphere these things imply; but we know what atmosphere they do imply. We recognize a certain note as natural and clear as the note of a bird; the note of St. Francis. There is in it something of gentle mockery of the very idea of possessions; something of a hope of disarming the enemy by generosity; something of a humorous sense of bewildering the worldly with the unexpected; something of the joy of carrying an enthusiastic conviction to a logical extreme. But anyhow we have no difficulty in recognizing it if we have read any of the literature of the Little Brothers and the movement that began in Assisi. It seems reasonable to infer that if it was this spirit that made such strange things possible in Umbria, it was the same spirit that made them possible in Palestine. If we hear the same unmistakable note and sense the same indescribable savor in two things at such a distance from each other, it seems natural to suppose that the case that is more remote from our experience was like the case that is closer to our experience. As the thing is explicable on the assumption that Francis was speaking to Franciscans, it is not an irrational explanation to suggest that Christ also was speaking to some dedicated band that had much the same function as Franciscans. In other words, it seems only natural to hold, as the Catholic Church has held, that these counsels of perfection were

part of a particular vocation to astonish and awaken
the world. But in any case it is important to note that
when we do find these particular features, with their
seemingly fantastic fitness, reappearing after more than
a thousand years, we find them produced by the same
religious system which claims continuity and authority from the scenes in which they first appeared. Any
number of philosophies will repeat the platitudes of
Christianity. But it is the ancient Church that can again
startle the world with the paradoxes of Christianity.
Ubi Petrus ibi Franciscus. ["Where there is Peter there is
Francis," a play on *Ubi Petrus ibi Ecclesia*, "Where there
is Peter there is the Church."]

But if we understand that it was truly under the
inspiration of his divine Master that St. Francis did
these merely quaint or eccentric acts of charity, we must
understand that it was under the same inspiration that
he did acts of self-denial and austerity. It is clear that
these more or less playful parables of the love of men
were conceived after a close study of the Sermon on the
Mount. But it is evident that he made an even closer
study of the silent sermon on that other mountain; the
mountain that was called Golgotha. Here again he was
speaking the strict historical truth, when he said that
in fasting or suffering humiliation he was but trying
to do something of what Christ did; and here again
it seems probable that as the same truth appears at
the two ends of a chain of tradition, the tradition has
preserved the truth. But the import of this fact at the
moment affects the next phase in the personal history
of the man himself.

For as it becomes clearer that his great communal
scheme is an accomplished fact and past the peril of an
early collapse, as it becomes evident that there already

is such a thing as an Order of the Friars Minor, this more individual and intense ambition of St. Francis emerges more and more. So soon as he certainly has followers, he does not compare himself with his followers, towards whom he might appear as a master; he compares himself more and more with his Master, towards whom he appears only as a servant. This, it may be said in passing, is one of the moral and even practical conveniences of the ascetical privilege. Every other sort of superiority may be superciliousness. But the saint is never supercilious, for he is always by hypothesis in the presence of a superior. The objection to an aristocracy is that it is a priesthood without a god. But in any case the service to which St. Francis had committed himself was one which, about this time, he conceived more and more in terms of sacrifice and crucifixion. He was full of the sentiment that he had not suffered enough to be worthy even to be a distant follower of his suffering God. And this passage in his history may really be roughly summarized as the Search for Martyrdom.

This was the ultimate idea in the remarkable business of his expedition among the Saracens in Syria. There were indeed other elements in his conception, which are worthy of more intelligent understanding than they have often received. His idea, of course, was to bring the Crusades in a double sense to their end; that is, to reach their conclusion and to achieve their purpose. Only he wished to do it by conversion and not by conquest; that is, by intellectual and not material means. The modern mind is hard to please; and it generally calls the way of Godfrey [Godfrey of Bouillon, Frankish knight and leader of the First Crusade] ferocious and the way of Francis fanatical. That is, it calls any moral method unpractical, when it has just called any practical method immoral. But the idea of St. Francis was far from being a fanatical or necessarily even an unpractical idea; though perhaps he saw the problem as rather too simple, lacking the learning of his great inheritor, Raymond Lully [Franciscan philosopher], who understood more but has been quite as little understood. The way he approached the matter was indeed highly personal and peculiar; but that was true of almost everything he did. It was in one way a simple idea, as most of his ideas were simple ideas. But it was not a silly idea; there was a great deal to be said for it and it might have succeeded. It was, of course, simply the idea that it is better to create Christians than to destroy Muslims. If Islam had been converted, the world would have been immeasurably more united and happy; for one thing, three quarters of the wars of modern history would never have taken place. It was not absurd to suppose that this might be affected, without military force, by missionaries who were also martyrs. The Church had conquered Europe in that way and may yet conquer Asia or Africa in that way. But when all this is allowed for, there is still another sense in which St. Francis was not thinking of Martyrdom as a means to an end, but almost as an end in itself; in the sense that to him the supreme end was to come closer to the example of Christ. Through all his plunging and, restless days ran the refrain: I have not suffered enough; I have not sacrificed enough; I am not yet worthy even of the shadow of the crown of thorns. He wandered about the valleys of the world looking for the hill that has the outline of a skull.

A little while before his final departure for the East a vast and triumphant assembly of the whole order had

been held near the Portiuncula [a small chapel near
Assisi, mother church of the young order]; and called
the Assembly of the Straw Huts, from the manner in
which that mighty army encamped in the field. Tradition says that it was on this occasion that St. Francis
met St. Dominic for the first and last time. It also says,
what is probable enough, that the practical spirit of
the Spaniard was almost appalled at the devout irre-
sponsibility of the Italian, who had assembled such a
crowd without organizing a commissariat. Dominic
the Spaniard was, like nearly every Spaniard, a man
with the mind of a soldier. His charity took the practical form of provision and preparation. But, apart from
the disputes about faith which such incidents open, he
probably did not understand in this case the power
of mere popularity produced by mere personality. In
all his leaps in the dark, Francis had an extraordinary
faculty of falling on his feet. The whole countryside
came down like a landslide to provide food and drink
for this sort of pious picnic. Peasants brought wagons
of wine and game; great nobles walked about doing
the work of footmen. It was a very real victory for the
Franciscan spirit of a reckless faith not only in God
but in man. Of course there is much doubt and dispute about the whole story and the whole relation of
Francis and Dominic; and the story of the Assembly
of the Straw Huts is told from the Franciscan side. But
the alleged meeting is worth mentioning, precisely
because it was immediately before St. Francis set forth
on his bloodless crusade that he is said to have met St.
Dominic, who has been so much criticized for lend-
ing himself to a more bloody one. There is no space
in this little book to explain how St. Francis, as much
as St. Dominic, would ultimately have defended the

defense of Christian unity by arms. Indeed it would
need a large book instead of a little book to develop
that point alone from its first principles. For the modern mind is merely a blank about the philosophy of
toleration; and the average agnostic of recent times
has really had no notion of what he meant by religious
liberty and equality. He took his own ethics as self-evident and enforced them; such as decency or the error
of the Adamite heresy. Then he was horribly shocked
if he heard of anybody else, Muslim or Christian, taking his ethics as self-evident and enforcing them; such
as reverence or the error of the Atheist heresy. And
then he wound up by taking all this lop-sided illogical
deadlock, of the unconscious meeting the unfamiliar,
and called it the liberality of his own mind. Medieval
men thought that if a social system was founded on a
certain idea it must fight for that idea, whether it was
as simple as Islam or as carefully balanced as Catholicism. Modern men really think the same thing, as is
clear when communists attack their ideas of property.
Only they do not think it so clearly, because they have
not really thought out their idea of property. But while
it is probable that St. Francis would have reluctantly
agreed with St. Dominic that war for the truth was
right in the last resort, it is certain that St. Dominic did
enthusiastically agree with St. Francis that it was far
better to prevail by persuasion and enlightenment if
it were possible. St. Dominic devoted himself much
more to persuading than to persecuting; but there was
a difference in the methods simply because there was a
difference in the men. About everything St. Francis did
there was something that was in a good sense childish,
and even in a good sense willful. He threw himself into
things abruptly, as if they had just occurred to him. He

made a dash for his Mediterranean enterprise with something of the air of a schoolboy running away to sea.

In the first act of that attempt he characteristically distinguished himself by becoming the Patron Saint of Stowaways. He never thought of waiting for introductions or bargains or any of the considerable backing that he already had from rich and responsible people. He simply saw a boat and threw himself into it, as he threw himself into everything else. It has all that air of running a race which makes his whole life read like an escapade or even literally an escape. He lay like lumber among the cargo, with one companion whom he had swept with him in his rush; but the voyage was apparently unfortunate and erratic and ended in an enforced return to Italy. Apparently it was after this first false start that the great reunion took place at the Portiuncula, and between this and the final Syrian journey there was also an attempt to meet the Muslim menace by preaching to the Moors in Spain. In Spain indeed several of the first Franciscans had already succeeded gloriously in being martyred. But the great Francis still went about stretching out his arms for such torments and desiring that agony in vain. No one would have said more readily than he that he was probably less like Christ than those others who had already found their Calvary; but the thing remained with him like a secret; the strangest of the sorrows of man.

His later voyage was more successful, so far as arriving at the scene of operations was concerned. He arrived at the headquarters of the Crusade which was in front of the besieged city of Damietta, and went on in his rapid and solitary fashion to seek the headquarters of the Saracens. He succeeded in

obtaining an interview with the Sultan; and it was at
that interview that he evidently offered, and as some
say proceeded, to fling himself into the fire as a divine
ordeal, defying the Muslim religious teachers to do
the same. It is quite certain that he would have done
so at a moment's notice. Indeed throwing himself
into the fire was hardly more desperate, in any case,
than throwing himself among the weapons and tools
of torture of a horde of fanatical Muslims and asking
them to renounce Muhammed. It is said further that
the Muslim muftis showed some coldness towards the
proposed competition, and that one of them quietly
withdrew while it was under discussion; which would
also appear credible. But for whatever reason Francis
evidently returned as freely as he came. There may be
something in the story of the individual impression
produced on the Sultan, which the narrator represents
as a sort of secret conversion. There may be something
in the suggestion that the holy man was unconsciously
protected among half-barbarous Orientals by the halo
of sanctity that is supposed in such places to surround
an idiot. There is probably as much or more in the more
generous explanation of that graceful though capri-
cious courtesy and compassion which mingled with
wilder things in the stately Sultans of the type and tradition of Saladin. Finally, there is perhaps something in
the suggestion that the tale of St. Francis might be told
as a sort of ironic tragedy and comedy called The Man
Who Could Not Get Killed. Men liked him too much
for himself to let him die for his faith; and the man
was received instead of the message. But all these are
only converging guesses at a great effort that is hard to
judge, because it broke off short like the beginnings of a

great bridge that might have united East and West, and remains one of the great might-have-beens of history.

Meanwhile the great movement in Italy was making giant strides. Backed now by papal authority as well as popular enthusiasm, and creating a kind of comradeship among all classes, it had started a riot of reconstruction on all sides of religious and social life; and especially began to express itself in that enthusiasm for building which is the mark of all the resurrections of Western Europe. There had notably been established at Bologna a magnificent mission house of the Friars Minor; and a vast body of them and their sympathizers surrounded it with a chorus of acclamation. Their unanimity had a strange interruption. One man alone in that crowd was seen to turn and suddenly denounce the building as if it had been a Babylonian temple; demanding indignantly since when the Lady Poverty had thus been insulted with the luxury of palaces. It was Francis, a wild figure, returned from his Eastern Crusade; and it was the first and last time that he spoke in wrath to his children.

A word must be said later about this serious division of sentiment and policy, about which many Franciscans, and to some extent Francis himself, parted company with the more moderate policy which ultimately prevailed. At this point we need only note it as another shadow fallen upon his spirit after his disappointment in the desert; and as in some sense the prelude to the next phase of his career, which is the most isolated and the most mysterious. It is true that everything about this episode seems to be covered with some cloud of dispute, even including its date; some writers putting it much earlier in the narrative than this. But whether or not it was chronologically it was certainly logically the culmination of the story, and may best be indicated here. I say indicated for it must be a matter of little more than indication; the thing being a mystery both in the higher moral and the more trivial historical sense. Anyhow the conditions of the affair seem to have been these. Francis and a young companion, in the course of their common wandering, came past a great castle all lighted up with the festivities attending a son of the house receiving the honor of knighthood. This aristocratic mansion . . . they entered in their beautiful and casual fashion and began to give their own sort of good news. There were some at least who listened to the saint "as if he had been an angel of God"; among them a gentleman named Orlando of Chiusi, who had great lands in Tuscany and who proceeded to do St. Francis a singular and somewhat picturesque act of courtesy. He gave him a mountain; a thing somewhat unique among the gifts of the world. Presumably the Franciscan rule which forbade a man to accept money had made no detailed provision about accepting mountains. Nor indeed did St. Francis accept it save as he accepted everything, as a temporary convenience rather than a personal possession; but he turned it into a sort of refuge for the eremitical rather than the monastic life; he retired there when he wished for a life of prayer and fasting which he did not ask even his closest friends to follow. This was Alverno of the Apennines, and upon its peak there rests forever a dark cloud that has a rim or halo of glory.

What it was exactly that happened there may never be known. The matter has been, I believe, a subject of dispute among the most devout students of the saintly life as well as between such students and others of the more secular sort. It may be that St. Francis never spoke to a soul on the subject; it would be highly characteristic, and it is certain in any case that he said very little; I think he is only alleged to have spoken of it to one man. Subject however to such truly sacred doubts, I will confess that to me personally this one solitary and indirect report that has come down to us reads very like the report of something real; of some of those things that are more real than what we call daily realities. Even something as it were double and bewildering about the image seems to carry the impression of an experience shaking the senses; as does the passage in Revelation about the supernatural creatures full of eyes. It would seem that St. Francis beheld the heavens above him occupied by a vast winged being like a seraph spread out like a cross. There seems some mystery about whether the winged figure was itself crucified or in the posture of crucifixion, or whether it merely enclosed in its frame of wings some colossal crucifix. But it seems clear that there was some question of the former impression; for St. Bonaventura distinctly says that St. Francis doubted how a seraph could be crucified, since those awful and ancient principalities were without the infirmity of the Passion. St. Bonaventure suggests that the seeming contradiction may have meant that St. Francis was to be crucified as a spirit since he could not be crucified as a man; but whatever the meaning of the vision, the general idea of it is very vivid and overwhelming. St. Francis saw above him, filling the whole heavens, some vast immemorial unthinkable power, ancient like the Ancient of Days, whose calm men had conceived under the forms of winged bulls or monstrous cherubim, and all that winged wonder was in pain like a wounded bird. This seraphic suffering, it is said, pierced his soul with a sword of grief and pity; it may be inferred that some sort of mounting agony accompanied the ecstasy. Finally after some fashion the apocalypse faded from the sky and the agony within subsided; and silence and the natural air filled the morning twilight and settled slowly in the purple chasms and cleft abysses of the Apennines. The head of the solitary sank, amid all that relaxation and quiet in which time can drift by with the sense of something ended and complete; and as he stared downwards, he saw the marks of nails in his own hands.

G

Gospel

The statement that the meek shall inherit the earth is very far from being a meek statement. I mean it is not meek in the ordinary sense of mild and moderate and inoffensive. To justify it, it would be necessary to go very deep into history and anticipate things undreamed of then and by many unrealized even now; such as the way in which the mystical monks reclaimed the lands which the practical kings had lost. If it was a truth at all, it was because it was a prophecy. But certainly it was not a truth in the sense of a truism. The blessing upon the meek would seem to be a very violent statement; in the sense of doing violence to reason and probability. And with this we come to another important stage in the speculation. As a prophecy it really was fulfilled; but it was only fulfilled long afterwards. The monasteries were the most practical and prosperous estates and experiments in reconstruction after the barbaric deluge; the meek did really inherit the earth. But nobody could have known anything of the sort at the time—unless indeed there was one who knew. Something of the same thing may be said about the incident of Martha and Mary, which has been interpreted in retrospect and from the inside by the mystics of the Christian contemplative life. But it was not at all an obvious view of it; and most moralists, ancient and modern, could be trusted to make a rush for the obvious. What torrents of effortless eloquence would have flowed from them to swell any slight superiority on the part of Martha; what splendid sermons about the Joy of Service and the Gospel of Work and the World Left Better Than We Found It, and generally all the ten thousand platitudes that can be uttered in favor of taking trouble—by people who need take no trouble to utter them. If in Mary the mystic and child of love Christ was guarding the seed of something more subtle, who was likely to understand it at the time? Nobody else could have seen Clare and Catherine and Teresa [saints of the Church who came later] shining above the little roof at Bethany. It is so in another way with that magnificent menace about bringing into the world a sword to sunder and divide. Nobody could have guessed then either how it could be fulfilled or how it could be justified. Indeed some freethinkers are still so simple as to fall into the trap and be shocked at a phrase so deliberately defiant. They actually complain of the paradox for not being a platitude.

But the point here is that if we could read the Gospel reports as things as new as newspaper reports, they would puzzle us and perhaps terrify us much more than the same things as developed by historical Christianity. For instance, Christ after a clear allusion to the eunuchs of eastern courts, said there would be eunuchs of the kingdom of heaven. If this does not mean the voluntary enthusiasm of virginity, it could only be made to mean something much more unnatural or uncouth. It is the historical religion that humanizes it for us by experience of Franciscans or of Sisters of Mercy. The mere statement standing by itself might very well suggest a rather dehumanized atmosphere; the sinister and inhuman silence of the Asiatic harem and divan. This is but one instance out of scores; but the moral is that the Christ of the Gospel might actually seem more strange and terrible than the Christ of the Church.

I am dwelling on the dark or dazzling or defiant or mysterious side of the Gospel words, not because they had not obviously a more obvious and popular side, but because this is the answer to a common criticism on a vital point. The freethinker frequently says that Jesus of Nazareth was a man of his time, even if he was in advance of his time; and that we cannot accept his ethics as final for humanity. The freethinker then goes on to criticize his ethics, saying plausibly enough that men cannot turn the other cheek, or that they must take thought for the morrow, or that the self-denial is too ascetic or the monogamy too severe. But the Zealots and the Legionaries did not turn the other cheek any more than we do, if so much. The Jewish traders and Roman tax-gatherers took thought for the morrow as much as we, if not more. We cannot pretend to be abandoning the morality of the past for one more suited to the present. It is certainly not the morality of another age, but it might be of another world.

In short, we can say that these ideals are impossible in themselves. Exactly what we cannot say is that they are impossible for us. . . .

H

Heretics

It is foolish, generally speaking, for a philosopher to set fire to another philosopher in Smithfield Market because they do not agree in their theory of the universe. That was done very frequently in the last decadence of the Middle Ages, and it failed altogether in its object. But there is one thing that is infinitely more absurd and unpractical than burning a man for his philosophy. This is the habit of saying that his philosophy does not matter, and this is done universally in the twentieth century, in the decadence of the great revolutionary period. General theories are everywhere condemned; the doctrine of the Rights of Man is dismissed with the doctrine of the Fall of Man. Atheism itself is too theological for us today. Revolution itself is too much of a system; liberty itself is too much of a restraint. We will have no generalizations. Mr. Bernard Shaw [George Bernard Shaw, Irish playwright and friend of GKC] has put the view in a perfect epigram: "The golden rule is that there is no golden rule." We are more and more to discuss details in art, politics, literature. A man's opinion on tramcars matters; his opinion on Botticelli matters; his opinion on all things does not matter. He may turn over and explore a million objects, but he must not find that strange object,

the universe; for if he does he will have a religion, and
be lost. Everything matters—except everything.

Examples are scarcely needed of this total levity
on the subject of cosmic philosophy. Examples are
scarcely needed to show that, whatever else we think
of as affecting practical affairs, we do not think it matters whether a man is a pessimist or an optimist, a Car-
tesian or a Hegelian, a materialist or a spiritualist. Let
me, however, take a random instance. At any innocent
tea-table we may easily hear a man say, "Life is not
worth living." We regard it as we regard the statement
that it is a fine day; nobody thinks that it can possibly
have any serious effect on the man or on the world.
And yet if that utterance were really believed, the
world would stand on its head. Murderers would be
given medals for saving men from life; firemen would
be denounced for keeping men from death; poisons
would be used as medicines; doctors would be called
in when people were well. . . . Yet we never specu-
late as to whether the conversational pessimist will
strengthen or disorganize society; for we are convinced
that theories do not matter.

This was certainly not the idea of those who introduced our freedom. When the old Liberals removed
the gags from all the heresies, their idea was that
religious and philosophical discoveries might thus
be made. Their view was that cosmic truth was so
important that everyone ought to bear independent
testimony. The modern idea is that cosmic truth is so
unimportant that it cannot matter what anyone says.
The former freed inquiry as men loose a noble hound;
the latter frees inquiry as men fling back into the sea
a fish unfit for eating. Never has there been so little
discussion about the nature of men as now, when, for

the first time, anyone can discuss it. The old restriction meant that only the orthodox were allowed to discuss religion. Modern liberty means that nobody is allowed to discuss it. Good taste, the last and vilest of human superstitions, has succeeded in silencing us where all the rest have failed. . . . It is still bad taste to be an avowed atheist. But their agony has achieved just this—that now it is equally bad taste to be an avowed Christian. . . .

But there are some people, nevertheless—and I am one of them—who think that the most practical and important thing about a man is still his view of the universe. We think that for a landlady considering a lodger, it is important to know his income, but still more important to know his philosophy. We think that for a general about to fight an enemy, it is important to know the enemy's numbers, but still more important to know the enemy's philosophy. We think the question is not whether the theory of the cosmos affects matters, but whether in the long run, anything else affects them. In the fifteenth century men cross-examined and tormented a man because he preached some immoral attitude; in the nineteenth century we feted and flattered Oscar Wilde because he preached such an attitude, and then broke his heart in penal servitude because he carried it out. It may be a question which of the two methods was the more cruel; there can be no kind of question which was the more ludicrous. The age of the Inquisition has not at least the disgrace of having produced a society which made an idol of the very same man for preaching the very same things which it made him a convict for practicing.

. . . For these reasons, and for many more, I for one have come to believe in going back to fundamentals. . . .

I wish to deal with my most distinguished contemporaries, not personally or in a merely literary manner, but in relation to the real body of doctrine which they teach. I am not concerned with Mr. Rudyard Kipling as a vivid artist or a vigorous personality; I am concerned with him as a Heretic—that is to say, a man whose view of things has the hardihood to differ from mine. I am not concerned with Mr. Bernard Shaw as one of the most brilliant and one of the most honest men alive; I am concerned with him as a Heretic—that is to say, a man whose philosophy is quite solid, quite coherent, and quite wrong. I revert to the doctrinal methods of the thirteenth century, inspired by the general hope of getting something done.

Suppose that a great commotion arises in the street about something, let us say a lamppost, which many influential persons desire to pull down. A gray-clad monk, who is the spirit of the Middle Ages, is approached upon the matter, and begins to say, in the arid manner of the Schoolmen [Scholastic theologians], "Let us first of all consider, my brethren, the value of Light. If Light be in itself good—." At this point he is somewhat excusably knocked down. All the people make a rush for the lamppost, the lamp-post is down in ten minutes, and they go about congratulating each other on their unmedieval practicality. But as things go on they do not work out so easily. Some people have pulled the lamp-post down because they wanted the electric light; some because they wanted old iron; some because they wanted darkness, because their deeds were evil. Some thought it not enough of a lamp-post, some too much; some acted because they wanted to smash municipal machinery; some because they wanted to smash something. And there is war in the night, no man knowing whom he strikes. So, gradually and inevitably, today, tomorrow, or the next day, there comes back the conviction that the monk was right after all, and that all depends on what is the philosophy of Light. Only what we might have discussed under the gas-lamp, we now must discuss in the dark.

I

Insanity

Thoroughly worldly people never understand even the
world; they rely altogether on a few cynical maxims
which are not true. Once I remember walking with
a prosperous publisher, who made a remark which I
had often heard before; it is, indeed, almost a motto of
the modern world. Yet I had heard it once too often,
and I saw suddenly that there was nothing in it. The
publisher said of somebody, "That man will get on; he
believes in himself." . . . I said to him. . . . "I know of
men who believe in themselves more colossally than
Napoleon or Caesar. I know where flames the fixed star
of certainty and success. I can guide you to the thrones
of the Supermen. The men who really believe in themselves are all in lunatic asylums." He said mildly that
there were a good many men after all who believed
in themselves and who were not in lunatic asylums.
"Yes, there are," I retorted, "and you of all men ought
to know them. That drunken poet from whom you
would not take a dreary tragedy, he believed in himself. That elderly minister with an epic from whom you
were hiding in a back room, he believed in himself.
If you consulted your business experience instead of
your ugly individualistic philosophy, you would know
that believing in himself is one of the commonest signs

59

of a rotter [cruel, stingy person]. Actors who can't act
believe in themselves; and debtors who won't pay. It
would be much truer to say that a man will certainly
fail because he believes in himself. Complete self-confidence is not merely a sin; complete self-confidence is a
weakness. Believing utterly in one's self is a hysterical
and superstitious belief. . . ." And to all this my friend
the publisher made this very deep and effective reply,
"Well, if a man is not to believe in himself, in what is
he to believe?" After a long pause I replied, "I will go
home and write a book in answer to that question."
This is the book that I have written in answer to it.

But I think this book may well start where our
argument started—in the neighborhood of the mad-
house. Modern masters of science are much impressed
with the need of beginning all inquiry with a fact.
The ancient masters of religion were quite equally
impressed with that necessity. They began with the
fact of sin—a fact as practical as potatoes. Whether or
not man could be washed in miraculous waters, there
was no doubt at any rate that he wanted washing. But
certain religious leaders in London, not mere materialists, have begun in our day not to deny the highly
disputable water, but to deny the indisputable dirt.
Certain new theologians dispute original sin, which is
the only part of Christian theology which can really be
proved. Some . . . in their almost too fastidious spiritualism, admit divine sinlessness, which they cannot see
even in their dreams. But they essentially deny human
sin, which they can see in the street. . . .

In this remarkable situation it is plainly not now
possible (with any hope of a universal appeal) to
start, as our fathers did, with the fact of sin. This very
fact which was to them (and is to me) as plain as a

pikestaff, is the very fact that has been specially diluted or denied. But though moderns deny the existence of sin, I do not think that they have yet denied the existence of a lunatic asylum. We all agree still that there is a collapse of the intellect as unmistakable as a falling house. . . . I mean that as all thoughts and theories were once judged by whether they tended to make a man lose his soul, so for our present purpose all modern thoughts and theories may be judged by whether they tend to make a man lose his wits.

It is true that some speak lightly and loosely of insanity as in itself attractive. But a moment's thought will show that if disease is beautiful, it is generally someone else's disease. A blind man may be picturesque; but it requires two eyes to see the picture. And similarly even the wildest poetry of insanity can only be enjoyed by the sane. To the insane man his insanity is quite prosaic, because it is quite true. A man who thinks himself a chicken is to himself as ordinary as a chicken. A man who thinks he is a bit of glass is to himself as dull as a bit of glass. It is the homogeneity of his mind which makes him dull, and which makes him mad. It is only because we see the irony of his idea that we think him even amusing; it is only because he does not see the irony of his idea that he is put in Hanwell at all. [Hanwell Insane Asylum lies eight miles west of central London.] In short, oddities only strike ordinary people. Oddities do not strike odd people. . . .

Let us begin, then, with the mad-house; from this evil and fantastic inn let us set forth on our intellectual journey. Now, if we are to glance at the philosophy of sanity, the first thing to do in the matter is to blot out one big and common mistake. There is a notion adrift everywhere that imagination, especially mystical imagination, is dangerous to man's mental balance. Poets are commonly spoken of as psychologically unreliable; and generally there is a vague association between wreathing laurels in your hair and sticking straws in it. Facts and history utterly contradict this view. Most of the very great poets have been not only sane, but extremely business-like; and if Shakespeare ever really held horses, it was because he was much the safest man to hold them. Imagination does not breed insanity. Exactly what does breed insanity is reason. Poets do not go mad; but chess-players do. Mathematicians go mad, and cashiers; but creative artists very seldom. I am not, as will be seen, in any sense attacking logic: I only say that this danger does lie in logic, not in imagination. Artistic paternity is as wholesome as physical paternity. Moreover, it is worthy of remark that when a poet really was morbid it was commonly because he had some weak spot of rationality on his brain. Poe, for instance, really was morbid; not because he was poetical, but because he was especially analytical. Even chess was too poetical for him; he disliked chess because it was full of knights and castles, like a poem. He avowedly preferred the black discs of draughts, because they were more like the mere black dots on a diagram. Perhaps the strongest case of all is this: that only one great English poet went mad, Cowper. And he was definitely driven mad by logic, by the ugly and alien logic of predestination. Poetry was not the disease, but the medicine; poetry partly kept him in health. He could sometimes forget the red and thirsty hell to which his hideous necessitarianism dragged him among the wide waters and the white flat lilies of the Ouse [a river in North Yorkshire, England]. He was damned by John Calvin; he was almost saved by John

Gilpin. Everywhere we see that men do not go mad by dreaming. Critics are much madder than poets. Homer is complete and calm enough; it is his critics who tear him into extravagant tatters. Shakespeare is quite himself; it is only some of his critics who have discovered that he was somebody else. And though St. John the Evangelist saw many strange monsters in his vision, he saw no creature so wild as one of his own commentators. The general fact is simple. Poetry is sane because it floats easily in an infinite sea; reason seeks to cross the infinite sea, and so make it finite. . . . That unmistakable mood or note that I hear from Hanwell, I hear also from half the chairs of science and seats of learning today; and most of the mad doctors are mad doctors in more senses than one. They all have exactly that combination we have noted: the combination of an expansive and exhaustive reason with a contracted common sense. They are universal only in the sense that they take one thin explanation and carry it very far. But a pattern can stretch forever and still be a small pattern. They see a chess-board white on black, and if the universe is paved with it, it is still white on black. Like the lunatic, they cannot alter their standpoint; they cannot make a mental effort and suddenly see it black on white.

Take first the more obvious case of materialism. As an explanation of the world, materialism has a sort of insane simplicity. It has just the quality of the madman's argument; we have at once the sense of it covering everything and the sense of it leaving everything out. Contemplate some able and sincere materialist . . . and you will have exactly this unique sensation. He understands everything, and everything does not seem worth understanding. His cosmos may be complete in every rivet and cog-wheel, but still his cosmos is smaller than our world. Somehow his scheme, like the lucid scheme of the madman, seems unconscious of the alien energies and the large indifference of the earth; it is not thinking of the real things of the earth, of fighting peoples or proud mothers, or first love or fear upon the sea. The earth is so very large, and the cosmos is so very small. The cosmos is about the smallest hole that a man can hide his head in.

. . . [W]e must remember that the materialist philosophy (whether true or not) is certainly much more limiting than any religion. In one sense, of course, all intelligent ideas are narrow. They cannot be broader than themselves. A Christian is only restricted in the same sense that an atheist is restricted. He cannot think Christianity false and continue to be a Christian; and the atheist cannot think atheism false and continue to be an atheist. But as it happens, there is a very special sense in which materialism has more restrictions than spirituality. Mr. McCabe [a materialist thinker and contemporary of GKC] thinks me a slave because I am not allowed to believe in determinism. I think Mr. McCabe a slave because he is not allowed to believe in fairies. But if we examine the two vetoes we shall see that his is really much more of a pure veto than mine. The Christian is quite free to believe that there is a considerable amount of settled order and inevitable development in the universe. But the materialist is not allowed to admit into his spotless machine the slightest speck of spirituality or miracle. Poor Mr. McCabe is not allowed to retain even the tiniest imp, though it might be hiding in a pimpernel. The Christian admits that the universe is manifold and even miscellaneous, just as a sane man knows that he is complex. The sane man knows that he has a touch of the beast, a touch of the devil, a touch of the saint, a touch of the citizen. Nay, the really sane man knows that he has a touch of the madman. But the materialist's world is quite simple and solid, just as the madman is quite sure he is sane. The materialist is sure that history has been simply and solely a chain of causation. . . . Materialists and madmen never have doubts.

Spiritual doctrines do not actually limit the mind as do materialistic denials. Even if I believe in immortality I need not think about it. But if I disbelieve in immortality I must not think about it. In the first case the road is open and I can go as far as I like; in the second the road is shut. But the case is even stronger, and the parallel with madness is yet more strange. For it was our case against the exhaustive and logical theory of the lunatic that, right or wrong, it gradually destroyed his humanity. Now it is the charge against the main deductions of the materialist that, right or wrong, they gradually destroy his humanity; I do not mean only kindness, I mean hope, courage, poetry, initiative, all that is human. For instance, when materialism leads men to complete fatalism (as it generally does), it is quite idle to pretend that it is in any sense a liberating force. It is absurd to say that you are especially advancing freedom when you only use free thought to destroy free will. The determinists come to bind, not to loose. They may well call their law the "chain" of causation. It is the worst chain that ever fettered a human being. You may use the language of liberty, if you like, about materialistic teaching, but it is obvious that this is just as inapplicable to it as a whole as the same language when applied to a man locked up in a mad-house. . . .

In passing from this subject I may note that there is a queer fallacy to the effect that materialistic fatalism is in some way favorable to mercy, to the abolition of cruel punishments or punishments of any kind. This is startlingly the reverse of the truth. It is quite tenable that the doctrine of necessity makes no difference at all; that it leaves the flogger flogging and the kind friend exhorting as before. But obviously if it stops either of them it stops the kind exhortation. That the sins are inevitable does not prevent punishment; if it prevents anything it prevents persuasion. Determinism is quite as likely to lead to cruelty as it is certain to lead to cowardice. Determinism is not inconsistent with the cruel treatment of criminals. What it is (perhaps) inconsistent with is the generous treatment of criminals; with any appeal to their better feelings or encouragement in their moral struggle. The determinist does not believe in appealing to the will, but he does believe in changing the environment. He must not say to the sinner, "Go and sin no more," because the sinner cannot help it. But he can put him in boiling oil; for boiling oil is an environment. Considered as a figure, therefore, the materialist has the fantastic outline of the figure of the madman. Both take up a position at once unanswerable and intolerable.

Of course it is not only of the materialist that all this is true. The same would apply to the other extreme of speculative logic. There is a skeptic far more terrible than he who believes that everything began in matter. It is possible to meet the skeptic who believes that everything began in himself. He doubts not the existence of angels or devils, but the existence of men and cows. For him his own friends are a mythology made up by himself. He created his own father and his own mother. This horrible fancy has in it something decidedly attractive to the somewhat mystical egoism of our day. That publisher who thought that men would get on if they believed in themselves, those seekers after the Superman who are always looking for him in the looking-glass, those writers who talk about impressing their personalities instead of creating life for the world, all these people have really only an inch between them and this awful emptiness. Then when this kindly world all around the man has been blackened out like a lie; when friends fade into ghosts, and the foundations of the world fail; then when the man, believing in nothing and in no man, is alone in his own nightmare, then the great individualistic motto shall be written over him in avenging irony. The stars will be only dots in the blackness of his own brain; his mother's face will be only a sketch from his own insane pencil on the walls of his cell. But over his cell shall be written, with dreadful truth, "He believes in himself."

J

St. Joan

A considerable time ago (at far too early an age, in fact) I read Voltaire's *La Pucelle* [*The Maid*, a satirical poem], a savage sarcasm on the traditional purity of Joan of Arc, very dirty, and very funny. I had not thought of it again for years, but it came back into my mind this morning because I began to turn over the leaves of the new *Jeanne d'Arc*, by that great and graceful writer, Anatole France. It is written in a tone of tender sympathy, and a sort of sad reverence; it never loses touch with a noble tact and courtesy, like that of a gentleman escorting a peasant girl through the modern crowd. It is invariably respectful to Joan, and even respectful to her religion. And being myself a furious admirer of Joan the Maid, I have reflectively compared the two methods, and I come to the conclusion that I prefer Voltaire's.

When a man of Voltaire's school has to explode a saint or a great religious hero, he says that such a person is a common human fool, or a common human fraud. But when a man like Anatole France has to explode a saint, he explains a saint as somebody belonging to his particular fussy little literary set. Voltaire read human nature into Joan of Arc, though it was only the brutal part of human nature. At least it was not specially Voltaire's nature. But M. France read M. France's nature into Joan of Arc—all the cold kindness, all the homeless sentimental sin of the modern literary man. There is one book that it recalled to me with startling vividness, though I have not seen the matter mentioned anywhere; Renan's *Vie de Jésus* [*Life of Jesus*—Ernest Renan, French philosopher and historian]. It has just the same general intention: that if you do not attack Christianity, you can at least patronize it. My own instinct, apart from my opinions, would be quite the other way. If I disbelieved in Christianity, I should be the loudest blasphemer in Hyde Park. Nothing ought to be too big for a brave man to attack; but there are some things too big for a man to patronize.

And I must say that the historical method seems to me excessively unreasonable. I have no knowledge of history, but I have as much knowledge of reason as Anatole France. And, if anything is irrational, it seems to me that the Renan-France way of dealing with miraculous stories is irrational. The Renan-France method is simply this: you explain supernatural stories that have some foundation simply by inventing natural stories that have no foundation. Suppose that you are confronted with the statement that Jack climbed up the beanstalk into the sky. It is perfectly philosophical to reply that you do not think that he did. It is (in my opinion) even more philosophical to reply that he may very probably have done so. But the Renan-France method is to write like this: "When we consider Jack's curious and even perilous heredity, which no doubt was derived from a female greengrocer and a profligate priest, we can easily understand how the ideas of heaven and a beanstalk came to be combined in his mind. Moreover, there is little doubt that he must have met some wandering conjurer from India, who told him about the tricks of the mango plant, and how it is sent up to the sky. We can imagine these two friends, the old man and the young, wandering in the woods together at evening, looking at the red and level clouds, as on that night when the old man pointed to a small beanstalk, and told his too imaginative companion that this also might be made to scale the heavens. And then, when we remember the quite exceptional psychology of Jack, when we remember how there was in him a union of the prosaic, the love of plain vegetables, with an almost irrelevant eagerness for the unattainable, for invisibility and the void, we shall no longer wonder that it was to him especially that was sent this sweet, though merely symbolic, dream of the tree uniting earth and heaven." That is the way that Renan and France write, only they do it better. But, really, a rationalist like myself becomes a little impatient and feels inclined to say, "But, hang it all, what do you know about the heredity of Jack or the psychology of Jack? You know nothing about Jack at all, except that some people say that he climbed up a beanstalk. Nobody would ever have thought of mentioning him if he hadn't. You must interpret him in terms of the beanstalk religion; you cannot merely interpret religion in terms of him. We have the materials of this story, and we can believe them or not. But we have not got the materials to make another story."

It is no exaggeration to say that this is the manner of M. Anatole France in dealing with Joan of Arc. Because her miracle is incredible to his somewhat old-fashioned materialism, he does not therefore dismiss it and her to fairyland with Jack and the Beanstalk. He tries to invent a real story, for which he can find no real evidence. He produces a scientific explanation which is quite destitute of any scientific proof. It is as if I (being entirely ignorant of botany and chemistry) said that the beanstalk grew to the sky because nitrogen and argon got into the subsidiary ducts of the corolla. To take the most obvious example, the principal character in M. France's story is a person who never existed at all. All Joan's wisdom and energy, it seems, came from a certain priest, of whom there is not the tiniest trace in all the multitudinous records of her life. The only foundation I can find for this fancy is the highly undemocratic idea that a peasant girl could not possibly have any ideas of her own. It is very hard for a freethinker to remain democratic. The writer seems altogether to forget what is meant by the moral atmosphere of a community. To say that Joan must have learnt her vision of a virgin overthrowing evil from *a* priest, is like saying that some modern girl in London, pitying the poor, must have learnt it from *a* Labor Member. She would learn it where the Labor Member learned it—in the whole state of our society.

But that is the modern method: the method of the reverent skeptic. When you find a life entirely incredible and incomprehensible from the outside, you pretend that you understand the inside. As Renan, the rationalist, could not make any sense out of Christ's most public acts, he proceeded to make an ingenious system out of His private thoughts. As Anatole France, on his own intellectual principle, cannot believe in what Joan of Arc did, he professes to be her dearest friend, and to know exactly what she meant. I cannot feel it to be a very rational manner of writing history; and sooner or later we shall have to find some more solid way of dealing with those spiritual phenomena with which all history is as closely spotted and spangled as the sky is with stars.

Joan of Arc is a wild and wonderful thing enough, but she is much saner than most of her critics and biographers. We shall not recover the common sense of Joan until we have recovered her mysticism. Our wars fail, because they begin with something sensible and obvious—such as getting to Pretoria by Christmas [reference to British military movements in the Second Boer War, 1899–1902]. But her war succeeded—because it began with something wild and perfect—the saints delivering France. She put her idealism in the right place, and her realism also in the right place: we moderns get both displaced. She put her dreams and her sentiment into her aims, where they ought to be; she put her practicality into her practice. In modern Imperial wars, the case is reversed. Our dreams, our aims are always, we insist, quite practical. It is our practice that is dreamy.

It is not for us to explain this flaming figure in terms of our tired and querulous culture. Rather we must try to explain ourselves by the blaze of such fixed stars. Those who called her a witch hot from hell were much more sensible than those who depict her as a silly sentimental maiden prompted by her parish priest. If I have to choose between the two schools of her scattered enemies, I could take my place with those subtle clerks who thought her divine mission devilish, rather than with those rustic aunts and uncles who thought it impossible.

K

Kensington High Street

If I have a native heath it is certainly Kensington High Street, off which stands the house of my childhood. I grew up in that thorough-fare which Mr. Max Beerbohm, with his usual easy exactitude of phrase, has described as "dapper, with a leaning to the fine arts." Dapper was never perhaps a descriptive term for myself; but it is quite true that I owe a certain taste for the arts to the sort of people among whom I was brought up. It is also true that such a taste, in various forms and degrees, was fairly common in the world which may be symbolized as Kensington High Street. And whether or not it is a tribute, it is certainly a truth that most people with an artistic turn in Kensington High Street would have been very much shocked, in their sense of propriety, if they had seen the popular shrines of Jerusalem; the sham gold, the garish colors, the fantastic tales and the feverish tumult. But what I want such people to do, and what they never do, is to turn this truth around. I want them to imagine, not a Kensington aesthete walking down David Street to the Holy Sepulchre, but a Greek monk or a Russian pilgrim walking down Kensington High Street to Kensington Gardens. I will not insist here on all the hundred plagues of plutocracy that would really surprise such a

Christian peasant; especially that curse of an irreligious society (unknown in religious societies, Muslim as well as Christian) the detestable denial of all dignity to the poor. I am not speaking now of moral but of artistic things; of the concrete arts and crafts used in popular worship. Well, my imaginary pilgrim would walk past Kensington Gardens till his sight was blasted by a prodigy. He would either fall on his knees as before a shrine, or cover his face as from a sacrilege. He would have seen the Albert Memorial. There is nothing so conspicuous in Jerusalem. There is nothing so gilded and gaudy in Jerusalem. Above all, there is nothing in Jerusalem that is on so large a scale and at the same time in so gay and glittering a style. My simple Eastern Christian would almost certainly be driven to cry aloud, "To what superhuman God was this enormous temple erected? I hope it is Christ; but I fear it is Antichrist." Such, he would think, might well be the great and golden image of the Prince of the World, set up in this great open space to receive the heathen prayers and heathen sacrifices of a lost humanity. I fancy he would feel a desire to be at home again amid the humble shrines of Zion. I really cannot imagine *what* he would feel, if he were told that the gilded idol was neither a god nor a demon, but a petty German prince who had some slight influence in turning us into the tools of Prussia.

Now I myself, I cheerfully admit, feel that enormity in Kensington Gardens as something quite natural. I feel it so because I have been brought up, so to speak, under its shadow; and stared at the graven images of Raphael and Shakespeare almost before I knew their names; and long before I saw anything funny in their figures being carved, on a smaller scale, under the feet of Prince Albert. I even took a certain childish pleasure in the gilding of the canopy and spire, as if in the golden palace of what was, to Peter Pan and all children, something of a fairy garden. So do the Christians of Jerusalem take pleasure, and possibly a childish pleasure, in the gilding of a better palace, besides a nobler garden, ornamented with a somewhat worthier aim. But the point is that the people of Kensington, whatever they might think about the Holy Sepulchre, do not think anything at all about the Albert Memorial. They are quite unconscious of how strange a thing it is; and that simply because they are used to it. The religious groups in Jerusalem are also accustomed to their colored background; and they are surely none the worse if they still feel rather more of the meaning of the colors. It may be said that they retain their childish illusion about *their* Albert Memorial. I confess I cannot manage to regard Palestine as a place where a special curse was laid on those who can become like little children. And I never could understand why such critics who agree that the kingdom of heaven is for children, should forbid it to be the only sort of kingdom that children would really like; a kingdom with real crowns of gold or even of tinsel. But that is another question, which I shall discuss in another place; the point is for the moment that such people would be quite as much surprised at the place of tinsel in our lives as we are at its place in theirs. If we are critical of the petty things they do to glorify great things, they would find quite as much to criticize (as in Kensington Gardens) in the great things we do to glorify petty things. And if we wonder at the way in which they seem to gild the lily, they would wonder quite as much at the way we gild the weed.

There are countless other examples of course of this principle of self-criticism, as the necessary condition of all criticism. . . . The worst superstition of Jerusalem, like the worst profligacy of Paris, is a thing so much invented for Anglo-Saxons that it might be called an Anglo-Saxon institution. But here again the critic could only really judge fairly if he realized with what abuses at home he ought really to compare this particular abuse abroad. He ought to imagine, for example, the feelings of a religious Russian peasant if he really understood all the highly-colored advertisements covering High Street Kensington Station. It is really not so repulsive to see the poor asking for money as to see the rich asking for more money. And advertisement is the rich asking for more money. A man would be annoyed if he found himself in a mob of millionaires, all holding out their silk hats for a penny; or all shouting with one voice, "Give me money." Yet advertisement does really assault the eye very much as such a shout would assault the ear. . . . It is a complete mistake to suppose that common people make our towns commonplace, with unsightly things like advertisements. Most of those whose wares are thus placarded everywhere are very wealthy gentlemen with coronets and country seats, men who are probably very particular about the artistic adornment of their own homes. They disfigure their towns in order to decorate their houses. To see such men crowding and clamoring for more wealth would really be a more unworthy sight than a scramble of poor guides; yet this is what would be conveyed by all the glare of gaudy advertisement to anybody who saw and understood it for the first time. Yet for us who are familiar with it all that gaudy advertisement fades into a background, just as the gaudy oriental patterns fade into a background for those oriental priests and pilgrims. Just as the innocent Kensington gentleman is wholly unaware that his black top hat is relieved against a background, or encircled as by a halo, of a yellow hoarding about mustard, so is the poor guide sometimes unaware that his small doings are dark against the fainter and more fading gold in which are traced only the humbler haloes of the Twelve Apostles.

L

Lying in Bed

Lying in bed would be an altogether perfect and supreme experience if only one had a colored pencil long enough to draw on the ceiling. This, however, is not generally a part of the domestic apparatus on the premises. . . . [I]f one worked in a really sweeping and masterly way, and laid on the color in great washes, it might drip down again on one's face in floods of rich and mingled color like some strange fairy rain; and that would have its disadvantages. I am afraid it would be necessary to stick to black and white in this form of artistic composition. To that purpose, indeed, the white ceiling would be of the greatest possible use; in fact, it is the only use I think of a white ceiling being put to.

But for the beautiful experiment of lying in bed I might never have discovered it. For years I have been looking for some blank spaces in a modern house to draw on. Paper is much too small for any really allegorical design. . . . But when I tried to find these fine clear spaces in the modern rooms such as we all live in I was continually disappointed. I found an endless pattern and complication of small objects hung like a curtain of fine links between me and my desire. I examined the walls; I found them to my surprise to be already covered with wallpaper, and I found the wallpaper

to be already covered with uninteresting images, all
bearing a ridiculous resemblance to each other. I could
not understand why one arbitrary symbol (a symbol
apparently entirely devoid of any religious or philosophical significance) should thus be sprinkled all over
my nice walls like a sort of smallpox. The Bible must be
referring to wallpapers, I think, when it says, "Use not
vain repetitions, as the Gentiles do." . . . Everywhere
that I went forlornly, with my pencil or my paint brush,
I found that others had unaccountably been before me,
spoiling the walls, the curtains, and the furniture with
their childish and barbaric designs.

Nowhere did I find a really clear space for sketching
until this occasion when I prolonged beyond the proper
limit the process of lying on my back in bed. Then the
light of that white heaven broke upon my vision, that
breadth of mere white which is indeed almost the definition of Paradise, since it means purity and also means
freedom. But alas! Like all heavens, now that it is seen
it is found to be unattainable; it looks more austere and
more distant than the blue sky outside the window.
For my proposal to paint on it with the bristly end of a
broom has been discouraged—never mind by whom; by
a person debarred from all political rights—and even
my minor proposal to put the other end of the broom
into the kitchen fire and turn it to charcoal has not been
conceded. Yet I am certain that it was from persons in
my position that all the original inspiration came for
covering the ceilings of palaces and cathedrals with
a riot of fallen angels or victorious gods. I am sure
that it was only because Michelangelo was engaged
in the ancient and honorable occupation of lying in
bed that he ever realized how the roof of the Sistine

Chapel might be made into an awful imitation of a divine drama that could only be acted in the heavens.

The tone now commonly taken toward the practice of lying in bed is hypocritical and unhealthy. Of all the marks of modernity that seem to mean a kind of decadence, there is none more menacing and dangerous that the exaltation of very small and secondary matters of conduct at the expense of very great and primary ones, at the expense of eternal ties and tragic human morality. If there is one thing worse that the modern weakening of major morals, it is the modern strengthening of minor morals. Thus it is considered more withering to accuse a man of bad taste than of bad ethics. Cleanliness is not next to godliness nowadays, for cleanliness is made essential and godliness is regarded as an offense. A playwright can attack the institution of marriage so long as he does not misrepresent the manners of society, and I have met an Ibsenite pessimist who thought it wrong to take beer but right to take prussic acid. Especially this is so in matters of hygiene; notably such matters as lying in bed. Instead of being regarded, as it ought to be, as a matter of personal convenience and adjustment, it has come to be regarded by many as if it were a part of essential morals to get up early in the morning. It is upon the whole part of practical wisdom; but there is nothing good about it or bad about its opposite.

Misers get up early in the morning; and burglars, I am informed, get up the night before. It is the great peril of our society that all its mechanisms may grow more fixed while its spirit grows more fickle. A man's minor actions and arrangements ought to be free, flexible, creative; the things that should be unchangeable are his principles, his ideals. But with us the reverse is true; our views change constantly; but our lunch does not change. Now, I should like men to have strong and rooted conceptions, but as for their lunch, let them have it sometimes in the garden, sometimes in bed, sometimes on the roof, sometimes in the top of a tree. Let them argue from the same first principles, but let them do it in a bed, or a boat, or a balloon. This alarming growth of good habits really means a too great emphasis on those virtues which mere custom can ensure, it means too little emphasis on those virtues which custom can never quite insure sudden and splendid virtues of inspired pity or of inspired candor. If ever that abrupt appeal is made to us we may fail. A man can get used to getting up at five o'clock in the morning. A man cannot very well get used to being burnt for his opinions; the first experiment is commonly fatal. Let us pay a little more attention to these possibilities of the heroic and unexpected. I dare say that when I get out of this bed I shall do some deed of an almost terrible virtue.

For those who study the great art of lying in bed there is one emphatic caution to be added. Even for those who can do their work in bed (like journalists), still more for those whose work cannot be done in bed (as, for example, the professional harpooners of whales), it is obvious that the indulgence must be very occasional. But that is not the caution I mean. The caution is this: if you do lie in bed, be sure you do it without any reason or justification at all. I do not speak, of course, of the seriously sick. But if a healthy man lies in bed, let him do it without a rag of excuse; then he will get up a healthy man. If he does it for some secondary hygienic reason, if he has some scientific explanation, he may get up a hypochondriac.

M

Miracles

A sketch of St. Francis of Assisi in modern English may be written in one of three ways. Between these the writer must make his selection; and the third way, which is adopted here, is in some respects the most difficult of all. At least, it would be the most difficult if the other two were not impossible.

First, he may deal with this great and most amazing man as a figure in secular history and a model of social virtues. He may describe this divine demagogue as being, as he probably was, the world's one quite sincere democrat. He may say (what means very little) that St. Francis was in advance of his age. He may say (what is quite true) that St. Francis anticipated all that is most liberal and sympathetic in the modern mood: the love of nature, the love of animals, the sense of social compassion, the sense of the spiritual dangers of prosperity and even of property. All those things that nobody understood before Wordsworth were familiar to St. Francis. All those things that were first discovered by Tolstoy could have been taken for granted by St Francis. He could be presented, not only as a human but a humanitarian hero; indeed as the first hero of humanism. He has been described as a sort of morning star of the Renaissance. And in comparison with

all these things, his ascetical theology can be ignored
or dismissed as a contemporary accident, which was
fortunately not a fatal accident. His religion can be
regarded as a superstition, but an inevitable superstition, from which not even genius could wholly free
itself; in the consideration of which it would be unjust
to condemn St. Francis for his self-denial or unduly
chide him for his chastity. It is quite true that even
from so detached a standpoint his stature would still
appear heroic. There would still be a great deal to be
said about the man who tried to end the Crusades by
talking to the Saracens or who interceded with the
Emperor for the birds. The writer might describe in
a purely historical spirit the whole of the Franciscan
inspiration that was felt in the painting of Giotto, in
the poetry of Dante, in the miracle plays that made
possible the modern drama, and in so many things
that are already appreciated by the modern culture. He
may try to do it, as others have done, almost without
raising any religious question at all. In short, he may
try to tell the story of a saint without God; which is like
being told to write the life of Nansen [Fridtjof Nansen,
Norwegian explorer and the first to reach 86°14' lati-
tude at the North Pole] and forbidden to mention the
North Pole.

Second, he may go to the opposite extreme, and
decide, as it were, to be defiantly devotional. He may
make the theological enthusiasm as thoroughly the
theme as it was the theme of the first Franciscans. He
may treat religion as the real thing that it was to the
real Francis of Assisi. He can find an austere joy, so to
speak, in parading the paradoxes of asceticism and all
the topsy-turveydom of humility. He can stamp the
whole history with the Stigmata, record fasts like fights

against a dragon; till in the vague modern mind St.
Francis is as dark a figure as St. Dominic. In short, he
can produce what many in our world will regard as a
sort of photographic negative; the reversal of all lights
and shades; what the foolish will find as impenetrable
as darkness and even many of the wise will find almost
as invisible as if it were written in silver upon white.
Such a study of St. Francis would be unintelligible to
anyone who does not share his religion, perhaps only
partly intelligible to anyone who does not share his
vocation. According to degrees of judgement, it will
be regarded as something too bad or too good for the
world. The only difficulty about doing the thing in this
way is that it cannot be done. It would really require
a saint to write about the life of a saint. In the present
case the objections to such a course are insuperable.

Third, he may try to do what I have tried to do
here; and as I have already suggested, the course has
peculiar problems of its own. The writer may put himself in the position of the ordinary modern outsider and
enquirer; as indeed the present writer is still largely
and was once entirely in that position. He may start
from the standpoint of a man who already admires St.
Francis, but only for those things which such a man
finds admirable. In other words he may assume that
the reader is at least as enlightened as Renan [Ernest
Renan, controversial author of *Life of Jesus*] or Matthew
Arnold; but in the light of that enlightenment he may
try to illuminate what Renan and Matthew Arnold left
dark. He may try to use what is understood to explain
what is not understood. He may try to say to the modern English reader: "Here is an historical character
which is admittedly attractive to many of us already,
by its gaiety, its romantic imagination, its spiritual

courtesy and camaraderie, but which also contains elements (evidently equally sincere and emphatic) which seem to you quite remote and repulsive. But after all, this man was a man and not half a dozen men. What seems inconsistency to you did not seem inconsistency to him. Let us see whether we can understand, with the help of the existing understanding, these other things that now seem to be doubly dark, by their intrinsic gloom and their ironic contrast." I do not mean, of course, that I can really reach a psychological completeness in this crude and curt outline. But I mean that this is the only controversial condition that I shall here assume; that I am dealing with the sympathetic outsider. I shall not assume any more or any less agreement than this. A materialist may not care whether the inconsistencies are reconciled or not. A Catholic may not see any inconsistencies to reconcile. But I am here addressing the ordinary common man, sympathetic but skeptical, and I can only rather hazily hope that, by approaching the great saint's story through what is evidently picturesque and popular about it, I may at least leave the reader understanding a little more than he did before of the consistency of a complete character; that by approaching it in this way, we may at least get a glimmering of why the poet who praised his lord the sun, often hid himself in a dark cavern, of why the saint who was so gentle with his Brother the Wolf was so harsh to his Brother the Ass (as he nicknamed his own body), of why the troubadour who said that love set his heart on fire separated himself from women, of why the singer who rejoiced in the strength and gaiety of the fire deliberately rolled himself in the snow, of why the very song which cries with all the passion of a pagan, "Praised be God for our Sister, Mother Earth, which brings forth varied fruits and grass and glowing flowers," ends almost with the words "Praised be God for our Sister, the death of the body."

Renan and Matthew Arnold failed utterly at this test. They were content to follow Francis with their praises until they were stopped by their prejudices; the stubborn prejudices of the sceptic. The moment Francis began to do something they did not understand or did not like, they did not try to understand, still less to like it; they simply turned their backs on the whole business and "walked no more with him." No man will get any further along a path of historical enquiry in that fashion. These skeptics are really driven to drop the whole subject in despair, to leave the most simple and sincere of all historical characters as a mass of contradiction, to be praised on the principle of the curate's egg. Arnold refers to the asceticism of Alverno [mountain where Francis received the stigmata] almost hurriedly, as if it were an unlucky but undeniable blot on the beauty of the story; or rather as if it were a pitiable breakdown and bathos at the end of story. Now this is simply to be stone-blind to the whole point of any story. To represent Mount Alverno as the mere collapse of Francis is exactly like representing Mount Calvary as the mere collapse of Christ. Those mountains are mountains, whatever else they are, and it is nonsense to say (like the Red Queen [a character in Lewis Carroll's *Through the Looking-Glass*]) that they are comparative hollows or negative holes in the ground. They were quite manifestly meant to be culminations and landmarks. To treat the Stigmata as a sort of scandal, to be touched on tenderly but with pain, is exactly like treating the original five wounds of Jesus Christ as five blots on his character. You may dislike the idea of asceticism; you may dislike equally the idea of martyrdom; for that matter you may have an honest and natural dislike of the whole conception of sacrifice symbolized by the cross. But if it is an intelligent dislike, you will retain the capacity for seeing the point of the story; the story of a martyr or even the story of a monk. You will not be able rationally to read the Gospel and regard the Crucifixion as an afterthought or an anti-climax or an accident in the life of Christ; it is obviously the point of the story like the point of a sword, the sword that pierced the heart of the Mother of God.

And you will not be able rationally to read the story of a man presented as a Mirror of Christ without understanding his final phase as a Man of Sorrows, and at least artistically appreciating the appropriateness of his receiving, in a cloud of mystery and isolation, inflicted by no human hand, the unhealed everlasting wounds that heal the world.

The practical reconciliation of the gaiety and austerity I must leave the story itself to suggest. But since I have mentioned Matthew Arnold and Renan and the rationalistic admirers of St. Francis, I will here give a hint of what it seems to me most advisable for such readers to keep in mind. These distinguished writers found things like the Stigmata a stumbling block because to them a religion was a philosophy. It was an impersonal thing; and it is only the most personal passion that provides here an approximate earthly parallel. A man will not roll in the snow for a stream of tendency by which all things fulfil the law of their being. He will not go without food in the name of something, not ourselves, that makes for righteousness. He will do things like this . . . under quite a different impulse. He

will do these things when he is in love. The first fact to
realize about St. Francis is involved with the first fact
with which his story starts; that when he said from
the first that he was a Troubadour, and said later that
he was a Troubadour of a newer and nobler romance,
he was not using a mere metaphor, but understood
himself much better than the scholars understand him.
He was, to the last agonies of asceticism, a Troubadour.
He was a Lover. He was a lover of God and he was
really and truly a lover of men; possibly a much rarer
mystical vocation. A lover of men is very nearly the
opposite of a philanthropist; indeed the pedantry of
the Greek word carries something like a satire on itself.
A philanthropist may be said to love anthropoids. But
as St. Francis did not love humanity but men, so he
did not love Christianity but Christ. Say, if you think
so, that he was a lunatic loving an imaginary person;
but an imaginary person, not an imaginary idea. And
for the modern reader the clue to the asceticism and
all the rest can be found in the stories of lovers when
they seemed to be rather like lunatics. Tell it as the
tale of one of the Troubadours, and the wild things he
would do for his lady, and the whole of the modern
puzzle disappears. In such a romance there would be
no contradiction between the poet gathering flowers
in the sun and enduring a freezing vigil in the snow,
between his praising all earthly and bodily beauty and
then refusing to eat, and between his glorifying gold
and purple and perversely going in rags, between his
showing pathetically a hunger for a happy life and a
thirst for a heroic death. All these riddles would be
easily resolved in the simplicity of any noble love;
only this was so noble a love that nine out of ten men
have hardly even heard of it. . . . [T]his parallel of the

earthly lover has a very practical relation to the problems of his life, as to his relations with his father and
his friends and their families. The modern reader will
almost always find that if he could only find this kind
of love as a reality, he could feel this kind of extrava-
gance as a romance. . . . The reader cannot even begin
to see the sense of a story that may well seem to him a
very wild one, until he understands that to this great
mystic his religion was not a thing like a theory but a
thing like a love affair. And the only purpose of this
prefatory chapter is to explain the limits of the present
book; which is only addressed to that part of the modern world which finds in St. Francis a certain modern
difficulty; which can admire him yet hardly accept him,
or which can appreciate the saint almost without the
sanctity. And my only claim even to attempt such a
task is that I myself have for so long been in various
stages of such a condition. Many thousand things that I
now partly comprehend I should have thought utterly
incomprehensible, many things I now hold sacred I
should have scouted as utterly superstitious, many
things that seem to me lucid and enlightened now they
are seen from the inside I should honestly have called
dark and barbarous seen from the outside, when long
ago in those days of boyhood my fancy first caught
fire with the glory of Francis of Assisi. I too have lived
in Arcady; but even in Arcady I met one walking in
a brown habit who loved the woods better than Pan.
The figure in the brown habit stands above the hearth
in the room where I write, and alone among many
such images, at no stage of my pilgrimage has he ever
seemed to me a stranger. There is something of a har-
mony between the hearth and the firelight and my own
first pleasure in his words about the brother fire; for he

stands far enough back in my memory to mingle with all those more domestic dreams of the first days. Even the fantastic shadows thrown by fire make a sort of shadow pantomime that belongs to the nursery; yet the shadows were even then the shadows of his favorite beast and birds, as he saw them, grotesque but haloed with the love of God. His Brother Wolf and Brother Sheep seemed then almost like the Brer Fox and Brer Rabbit of a more Christian Uncle Remus. I have come slowly to see many more marvelous aspects of such a man, but I have never lost that one. His figure stands on a sort of bridge connecting my boyhood with my conversion to many other things; for the romance of his religion has penetrated even the rationalism of that vague Victorian time. In so far as I have had this experience, I may be able to lead others a little further along that road; but only a very little further. Nobody knows better than I do now that it is a road upon which angels might fear to tread; but though I am certain of failure I am not altogether overcome by fear; for he suffered fools gladly.

N

Negativity

Much has been said, and said truly, of the monkish morbidity, of the hysteria which has often gone with the visions of hermits or nuns. But let us never forget that this visionary religion is, in one sense, necessarily more wholesome than our modern and reasonable morality. It is more wholesome for this reason, that it can contemplate the idea of success or triumph in the hopeless fight towards the ethical ideal. . . . A modern morality, on the other hand, can only point with absolute conviction to the horrors that follow breaches of law; its only certainty is a certainty of ill. It can only point to imperfection. It has no perfection to point to. But the monk meditating upon Christ or Buddha has in his mind an image of perfect health, a thing of clear colors and clean air. He may contemplate this ideal wholeness and happiness far more than he ought; he may contemplate it to the neglect or exclusion of essential things; he may contemplate it until he has become a dreamer or a driveller; but still it is wholeness and happiness that he is contemplating. He may even go mad; but he is going mad for the love of sanity. But the modern student of ethics, even if he remains sane, remains sane from an insane dread of insanity.

The anchorite rolling on the stones in a frenzy of submission is a healthier person fundamentally than many a sober man in a silk hat who is walking down Cheapside. For many such are good only through a withering knowledge of evil. I am not at this moment claiming for the devotee anything more than this primary advantage, that though he may be making himself personally weak and miserable, he is still fixing his thoughts largely on gigantic strength and happiness, on a strength that has no limits, and a happiness that has no end. Doubtless there are other objections which can be urged without unreason against the influence of gods and visions in morality, whether in the cell or street. But this advantage the mystic morality must always have—it is always jollier. A young man may keep himself from vice by continually thinking of disease. He may keep himself from it also by continually thinking of the Virgin Mary. There may be question about which method is the more reasonable, or even about which is the more efficient. But surely there can be no question about which is the more wholesome.

I remember a pamphlet . . . which contained a phrase sharply symbolizing and dividing these two methods. The pamphlet was called *Beer and Bible* . . . two very noble things . . . which I confess to thinking appropriate and charming. I have not the work by me, but I remember that Mr. Foote [its author] dismissed very contemptuously any attempts to deal with the problem of strong drink by religious offices or intercessions, and said that a picture of a drunkard's liver would be more efficacious in the matter of temperance than any prayer or praise. In that picturesque expression, it seems to me, is perfectly embodied the incurable morbidity of modern ethics. In that temple the lights are low, the crowds kneel, the solemn anthems are uplifted. But that upon the altar to which all men kneel is no longer the perfect flesh, the body and substance of the perfect man; it is still flesh, but it is diseased. It is the drunkard's liver of the New Testament that is marred for us, which we take in remembrance of him.

Now, it is this great gap in modern ethics, the absence of vivid pictures of purity and spiritual triumph, which lies at the back of the real objection felt by so many sane men to the realistic literature of the nineteenth century. If any ordinary man ever said that he was horrified by the subjects discussed in Ibsen or Maupassant [Henrik Ibsen, Norwegian playwright; Guy de Maupassant, French fiction writer; both naturalists and pessimists], or by the plain language in which they are spoken of, that ordinary man was lying. The average conversation of average men throughout the whole of modern civilization in every class or trade is such as Zola [Émile Zola, French writer, with a similar reputation to Ibsen's and Maupassant's] would never dream of printing. Nor is the habit of writing thus of these things a new habit. On the contrary, it is the Victorian prudery and silence which is new still, though it is already dying. The tradition of calling a spade a spade starts very early in our literature and comes down very late. But the truth is that the ordinary honest man, whatever vague account he may have given of his feelings, was not either disgusted or even annoyed at the candor of the moderns. What disgusted him, and very justly, was not the presence of a clear realism, but the absence of a clear idealism. Strong and genuine religious sentiment has never had any objection to realism; on the contrary, religion was the realistic thing, the brutal thing, the thing that called names. This is the great difference between some recent developments of Nonconformity and the great Puritanism of the seventeenth century. It was the whole point of the Puritans that they cared nothing for decency. Modern Nonconformist newspapers distinguish themselves by suppressing precisely those nouns and adjectives which the founders of Nonconformity distinguished themselves by flinging at kings and queens. But if it was a chief claim of religion that it spoke plainly about evil, it was the chief claim of all that it spoke plainly about good. The thing which is resented, and, as I think, rightly resented . . . is that while the eye that can perceive what are the wrong things increases in an uncanny and devouring clarity, the eye which sees what things are right is growing mistier and mistier every moment, till it goes almost blind with doubt. If we compare, let us say, the morality of the *Divine Comedy* with the morality of Ibsen's *Ghosts*, we shall see all that modern ethics have really done. No one, I imagine, will accuse the author of the *Inferno* of an Early Victorian prudishness. . . . But Dante describes three moral instruments—Heaven, Purgatory, and Hell, the vision of perfection, the vision of improvement, and the vision of failure. Ibsen has only one—Hell. It is often said, and with perfect truth, that no one could read a play like *Ghosts* and remain indifferent to the necessity of an ethical self-command. That is quite true, and the same is to be said of the most monstrous and material descriptions of the eternal fire. It is quite certain the realists like Zola do in one sense promote morality—they promote it in the sense in which the hangman promotes it, in the sense in which the devil promotes it. But they only affect that small

minority which will accept any virtue of courage. Most
healthy people dismiss these moral dangers as they
dismiss the possibility of bombs or microbes. Modern
realists are indeed Terrorists, like the dynamiters; and
they fail just as much in their effort to create a thrill.
Both realists and dynamiters are well-meaning people
engaged in the task, so obviously ultimately hopeless,
of using science to promote morality.

. . . [T]his absence of a permanent key to virtue,
is the one great Ibsen merit. I am not discussing now
with any fullness whether this is so or not. All I ven-
ture to point out, with an increased firmness, is that
this omission, good or bad, does leave us face to face
with the problem of a human consciousness filled with
very definite images of evil, and with no definite image
of good. To us light must be henceforward the dark
thing—the thing of which we cannot speak. To us, as to
Milton's devils in Pandemonium [John Milton, author
of *Paradise Lost*, an epic poem in which Pandemonium
is the capital of Hell], it is darkness that is visible. The
human race, according to religion, fell once, and in
falling gained knowledge of good and of evil. Now we
have fallen a second time, and only the knowledge of
evil remains to us.

O

Orthodoxy

All Christianity concentrates on the man at the cross-roads. The vast and shallow philosophies, the huge syntheses of humbug, all talk about ages and evolution and ultimate developments. The true philosophy is concerned with the instant. Will a man take this road or that?—that is the only thing to think about, if you enjoy thinking. The eons are easy enough to think about, anyone can think about them. The instant is really awful: and it is because our religion has intensely felt the instant, that it has in literature dealt much with battle and in theology dealt much with hell. It is full of danger, like a boy's book: it is at an immortal crisis. There is a great deal of real similarity between popular fiction and the religion of the western people. If you say that popular fiction is vulgar and tawdry, you only say what the dreary and well-informed say also about the images in the Catholic churches. Life (according to the faith) is very like a serial story in a magazine: life ends with the promise (or menace) "to be continued in our next." Also, with a noble vulgarity, life imitates the serial and leaves off at the exciting moment. For death is distinctly an exciting moment.

But the point is that a story is exciting because it has in it so strong an element of will, of what theology calls free-will. You cannot finish a sum how you like. But you can finish a story how you like. When somebody discovered the Differential Calculus there was only one Differential Calculus he could discover. But when Shakespeare killed Romeo he might have married him to Juliet's old nurse if he had felt inclined. And Christendom has excelled in the narrative romance exactly because it has insisted on the theological free-will. It is a large matter and too much to one side of the road to be discussed adequately here; but this is the real objection to that torrent of modern talk about treating crime as disease, about making a prison merely a hygienic environment like a hospital, of healing sin by slow scientific methods. The fallacy of the whole thing is that evil is a matter of active choice whereas disease is not. If you say that you are going to cure a profligate as you cure an asthmatic, my cheap and obvious answer is, "Produce the people who want to be asthmatics as many people want to be profligates." A man may lie still and be cured of a malady. But he must not lie still if he wants to be cured of a sin; on the contrary, he must get up and jump about violently. The whole point indeed is perfectly expressed in the very word which we use for a man in hospital; "patient" is in the passive mood; "sinner" is in the active. If a man is to be saved from influenza, he may be a patient. But if he is to be saved from forging, he must be not a patient but an impatient. He must be personally impatient with forgery. All moral reform must start in the active not the passive will.

Here again we reach the same substantial conclusion. In so far as we desire the definite reconstructions and the dangerous revolutions which have distinguished European civilization, we shall not discourage the thought of possible ruin; we shall rather encourage it. If we want, like the Eastern saints, merely to contemplate how right things are, of course we shall only say that they must go right. But if we particularly want to make them go right, we must insist that they may go wrong.

Lastly, this truth is yet again true in the case of the common modern attempts to diminish or to explain away the divinity of Christ. The thing may be true or not; that I shall deal with before I end. But if the divinity is true it is certainly terribly revolutionary. That a good man may have his back to the wall is no more than we knew already; but that God could have his back to the wall is a boast for all insurgents forever. Christianity is the only religion on earth that has felt that omnipotence made God incomplete. Christianity alone has felt that God, to be wholly God, must have been a rebel as well as a king. Alone of all creeds, Christianity has added courage to the virtues of the Creator. For the only courage worth calling courage must necessarily mean that the soul passes a breaking point—and does not break. In this indeed I approach a matter more dark and awful than it is easy to discuss; and I apologize in advance if any of my phrases fall wrong or seem irreverent touching a matter which the greatest saints and thinkers have justly feared to approach. But in that terrific tale of the Passion there is a distinct emotional suggestion that the author of all things (in some unthinkable way) went not only through agony, but through doubt. It is written, "Thou shalt not tempt the Lord thy God." No; but the Lord thy God may tempt Himself; and it seems as if this was what happened in Gethsemane. In a garden Satan tempted man: and in a garden God tempted God. He passed in some superhuman manner through our human horror of pessimism. When the world shook and the sun was wiped out of heaven, it was not at the crucifixion, but at the cry from the cross: the cry which confessed that God was forsaken of God. And now let the revolution-ists choose a creed from all the creeds and a god from all the gods of the world, carefully weighing all the gods of inevitable recurrence and of unalterable power. They will not find another god who has himself been in revolt. Nay, (the matter grows too difficult for human speech,) but let the atheists themselves choose a god. They will find only one divinity who ever uttered their isolation; only one religion in which God seemed for an instant to be an atheist.

These can be called the essentials of the old ortho-doxy, of which the chief merit is that it is the natu-ral fountain of revolution and reform; and of which the chief defect is that it is obviously only an abstract assertion. Its main advantage is that it is the most adventurous and manly of all theologies. Its chief dis-advantage is simply that it is a theology. It can always be urged against it that it is in its nature arbitrary and in the air. But it is not so high in the air but that great archers spend their whole lives in shooting arrows at it—yes, and their last arrows; there are men who will ruin themselves and ruin their civilization if they may ruin also this old fantastic tale. This is the last and most astounding fact about this faith; that its enemies will use any weapon against it, the swords that cut their own fingers, and the firebrands that burn their own homes. Men who begin to fight the Church for the sake of freedom and humanity end by flinging away free-dom and humanity if only they may fight the Church. This is no exaggeration; I could fill a book with the instances of it. Mr. Blatchford [Robert Blatchford, prominent atheist and journalist and contemporary of GKC] set out, as an ordinary Bible-smasher, to prove that Adam was guiltless of sin against God; in maneuvering so as to maintain this he admitted, as a mere side issue, that all the tyrants, from Nero to King Leopold, were guiltless of any sin against humanity. I know a man who has such a passion for proving that he will have no personal existence after death that he falls back on the position that he has no personal existence now. He invokes Buddhism and says that all souls fade into each other; in order to prove that he cannot go to heaven he proves that he cannot go to Hartlepool [a town on the North Sea coast of England]. I have known people who protested against religious education with arguments against any education, saying that the child's mind must grow freely or that the old must not teach the young. I have known people who showed that there could be no divine judgment by showing that there can be no human judgment, even for practical purposes. They burned their own corn to set fire to the church; they smashed their own tools to smash it; any stick was good enough to beat it with, though it were the last stick of their own dismembered furniture. We do not admire, we hardly excuse, the fanatic who wrecks this world for love of the other. But what are we to say of the fanatic who wrecks this world out of hatred of the other? He sacrifices the very existence of humanity to the non-existence of God. He offers his victims not to the altar, but merely to assert the idleness of the altar and the emptiness of the throne. He is ready to ruin even that primary ethic by which all things live, for his strange and eternal vengeance upon someone who never lived at all.

And yet the thing hangs in the heavens unhurt. Its opponents only succeed in destroying all that they themselves justly hold dear. They do not destroy orthodoxy; they only destroy political courage and common sense. They do not prove that Adam was not responsible to God; how could they prove it? They only prove (from their premises) that the Czar is not responsible to Russia. They do not prove that Adam should not have been punished by God; they only prove that the nearest sweater should not be punished by men. With their oriental doubts about personality they do not make certain that we shall have no personal life hereafter; they only make certain that we shall not have a very jolly or complete one here. With their paralyzing hints of all conclusions coming out wrong they do not tear the book of the Recording Angel; they only make it a little harder to keep the books of Marshall & Snelgrove [a department store once located on Oxford Street, London]. Not only is the faith the mother of all worldly energies, but its foes are the fathers of all worldly confusion. The secularists have not wrecked divine things; but the secularists have wrecked secular things, if that is any comfort to them. The Titans did not scale heaven; but they laid waste the world.

P

Primitive Revelation

There is at the back of all our lives an abyss of light, more blinding and unfathomable than any abyss of darkness; and it is the abyss of actuality, of existence, of the fact that things truly are, and that we ourselves are incredibly and sometimes almost incredulously real. It is the fundamental fact of being, as against not being; it is unthinkable, yet we cannot unthink it, though we may sometimes be unthinking about it; unthinking and especially unthanking. For he who has realized this reality knows that it does outweigh, literally to infinity, all lesser regrets or arguments for negation, and that under all our grumblings there is a subconscious substance of gratitude. That light of the positive is the business of the poets, because they see all things in the light of it more than do other men. Chaucer was a child of light and not merely of twilight, the mere red twilight of one passing dawn of revolution, or the gray twilight of one dying day of social decline. He was the immediate heir of something like what Catholics call the Primitive Revelation; that glimpse that was given of the world when God saw that it was good; and so long as the artist gives us glimpses of that, it matters nothing that they are fragmentary or even trivial; whether it be in the mere fact that a medieval

Court poet could appreciate a daisy, or that he could write, in a sort of flash of blinding moonshine, of the lover who "slept no more than does the nightingale." These things belong to the same world of wonder as the primary wonder at the very existence of the world; higher than any common pros and cons, or likes and dislikes, however legitimate. Creation was the greatest of all Revolutions. It was for that, as the ancient poet said, that the morning stars sang together; and the most modern poets, like the medieval poets, may descend very far from that height of realization and stray and stumble and seem distraught; but we shall know them for the Sons of God, when they are still shouting for joy. This is something much more mystical and absolute than any modern thing that is called optimism; for it is only rarely that we realize, like a vision of the heavens filled with a chorus of giants, the primeval duty of Praise.

Q

Questing

There is, then, something to be said for the long poetical allegories eventually abandoned by Chaucer; as for the long prose romances ultimately satirized by Cervantes. Their very extension and expanse satisfied a psychological need now perhaps only felt by children and poor people, who like to have a very big book for their money. Yet there are few cultivated moderns who have not felt something of the pleasure of being able to lose themselves in the longest books of Dickens or Trollope. But there is more in it than that; for man lives by his devouring appetite for morality. The chivalric romance does really represent the Christian conception of life, which is at once a Quest, a Test and an Adventure. And the decorative allegories, that seem so dead to us, were once alive like a dance with the balanced morality of the Middle Ages.

Dante makes the very heavens dance, in the last pages of the *Paradiso* [book three of Dante's *Divine Comedy*, about Heaven]; sweeping the sky with swaying and spinning ballets of angels and spirits; and the symbol is very appropriate to the philosophy. It is appropriate; not because the dance stands for disorder, but because it stands for order. The dance is in its nature a rhythmic and recurrent thing, returning

upon itself; and was therefore a perfectly correct and
orthodox type of medieval moral theology. This, by
the way, will be noted by the intelligent as correcting
the exaggerated solemnity, with which some scholars have taken the tirades of fanatical friars, and other
people, against the use or abuse of dancing. Doubtless
there was much that was really pagan left in popular
dancing, and doubtless there were plenty of donkeys
in holy orders who found paganism in what was not
really pagan. But in face of a fact like Dante's vision
of the celestial dance, it is not tenable that the medieval mind thought of dancing merely as immorality or
indecency. Nobody would describe people as doing in
heaven what he had a deep and indignant horror of
their doing on earth. Muhammed would not describe
his Paradise as a place where the faithful were incessantly occupied in carving and worshiping idols. The
Pacifist would not point happily to a future life in
which everybody would be always waving sabers and
firing off guns; the Prohibitionist would not picture
heaven as a state of perfection in which the blessed
could drink rum and gin for ever and ever. And Dante
would not have filled the skies with dancing, if he had
instinctively thought of the dance as degrading. The
truth is, of course, that he instinctively thought of the
dance as decorative and rhythmic, and therefore corre-
sponding to a certain character in his whole conception
of life. Indeed, it marks the whole difference between
medieval life and modern life.

A certain break or sharp change in history can
hardly be sketched more sharply, than by saying that
up to a certain time life was conceived as a Dance, and
after that time life was conceived as a Race. Medieval morality was full of the idea that one thing must

balance another, that each stood on one side or the other of something that was in the middle, and something that remained in the middle. There might be any amount of movement, but it was movement round this central thing; perpetually altering the attitudes, but perpetually preserving the balance. The Virtues were like children going round the Mulberry Bush, only the Mulberry Bush was that Burning Bush which they made symbolical of the Incarnation; that flamboyant bush in which the Virgin and Child appear in the picture, with Rene of Provence [fifteenth-century king of Naples and patron of arts] and his beloved wife kneeling on either side. Now since that break in history, whatever we call it or whatever we think of it, the Dance has turned into a Race. That is, the dancers lose their balance and only recover it by running towards some object, or alleged object; not an object within their circle or their possession, but an object which they do not yet possess. It is a flying object; a disappearing object; and, as some hold, a disappointing object. But I am not concerned with condemning or commending either the religion of the Race or the religion of the Dance. I am only pointing out that this is the fundamental difference between them. One is rhythmic and recurrent movement, because there is a known center; while the other is precipitate or progressive movement, because there is an unknown goal. The latter has produced all that we call Progress; the former produced what the medievals meant by Order; but it was the lively order of a dance.

R

Religions Compared

Comparative religion is very comparative indeed. That is, it is so much a matter of degree and distance and difference that it is only comparatively successful when it tries to compare. When we come to look at it closely we find it comparing things that are really quite incomparable. We are accustomed to see a table or catalogue of the world's great religions in parallel columns, until we fancy they are really parallel. We are accustomed to see the names of the great religious founders all in a row: Christ; Muhammed; Buddha; Confucius. But in truth this is only a trick, another of these optical illusions by which any objects may be put into a particular relation by shifting to a particular point of sight. Those religions and religious founders, or rather those whom we choose to lump together as religions and religious founders, do not really show any common character. The illusion is partly produced by Islam coming immediately after Christianity in the list; as Islam did come after Christianity and was largely an imitation of Christianity. But the other eastern religions, or what we call religions, not only do not resemble the Church but do not resemble each other. When we come to Confucianism at the end of the list, we come to something in a totally different world of thought. To compare the

Christian and Confucian religions is like comparing
a theist with an English squire or asking whether a
man is a believer in immortality or a hundred-per-cent
American. Confucianism may be a civilization but it
is not a religion.

In truth the Church is too unique to prove herself
unique. For most popular and easy proof is by parallel;
and here there is no parallel. It is not easy, therefore,
to expose the fallacy by which a false classification is
created to swamp a unique thing, when it really is a
unique thing. As there is nowhere else exactly the same
fact, so there is nowhere else exactly the same fallacy.
But I will take the nearest thing I can find to such a
solitary social phenomenon, in order to show how it
is thus swamped and assimilated. I imagine most of
us would agree that there is something unusual and
unique about the position of the Jews. There is nothing
that is quite in the same sense an international nation;
an ancient culture scattered in different countries but
still distinct and indestructible. Now this business is
like an attempt to make a list of Nomadic Nations in
order to soften the strange solitude of the Jew. It would
be easy enough to do it, by the same process of putting
a plausible approximation first, and then tailing off into
totally different things thrown in somehow to make
up the list. Thus in the new list of nomadic nations
the Jews would be followed by the Gypsies; who at
least are really nomadic if they are not really national.
Then the professor of the new science of Comparative
Nomadics could pass easily on to something different;
even if it was very different. He could remark on the
wandering adventure of the English who had scattered their colonies over so many seas; and call them
nomads. It is quite true that a great many Englishmen

seem to be strangely restless in England. It is quite true that not all of them have left their country for their country's good. The moment we mention the wandering empire of the English, we must add the strange exiled empire of the Irish. For it is a curious fact, to be noted in our imperial literature, that the same ubiquity and unrest which is a proof of English enterprise and triumph is a proof of Irish futility and failure. Then the professor of Nomadism would look round thoughtfully and remember that there was great talk recently of German waiters, German barbers, German clerks, Germans naturalizing themselves in England and the United States and the South American republics. The Germans would go down as the fifth nomadic race; the words Wanderlust and Folk-Wandering would come in very useful here. For there really have been historians who explained the Crusades by suggesting that the Germans were found wandering (as the police say) in what happened to be the neighborhood of Palestine. Then the professor, feeling he was now near the end, would make a last leap in desperation. He would recall the fact that the French army has captured nearly every capital in Europe, that it marched across countless conquered lands under Charlemagne or Napoleon; and that would be wanderlust and that would be the note of a nomadic race. Thus he would have his six nomadic nations all compact and complete, and would feel that the Jew was no longer a sort of mysterious and even mystical exception. But people with more common sense would probably realize that he had only extended nomadism by extending the meaning of nomadism, and that he had extended that until it really had no meaning at all. It is quite true that the French soldier has made some of the finest marches in all military history. But it is equally true, and far more self-evident, that if the French peasant is not a rooted reality there is no such thing as a rooted reality in the world; or in other words, if he is a nomad there is nobody who is not a nomad.

Now that is the sort of trick that has been tried in the case of comparative religion and the world's religious founders all standing respectably in a row. It seeks to classify Jesus as the other would classify Jews, by inventing a new class for the purpose and filling up the rest of it with stop-gaps and second-rate copies. I do not mean that these other things are not often great things in their own real character and class. Confucianism and Buddhism are great things, but it is not true to call them Churches; just as the French and English are great peoples, but it is nonsense to call them nomads. There are some points of resemblance between Christendom and its imitation in Islam; for that matter there are some points of resemblance between Jews and Gypsies. But after that the lists are made up of anything that comes to hand; of anything that can be put in the same catalogue without being in the same category.

In this sketch of religious history, with all decent deference to men much more learned than myself, I propose to cut across and disregard this modern method of classification, which I feel sure has falsified the facts of history. I shall here submit an alternative classification of religion or religions, which I believe would be found to cover all the facts and, what is quite as important here, all the fancies. Instead of dividing religion geographically and as it were vertically, into Christian, Muslim, Brahman, Buddhist, and so on, I would divide it psychologically and in some sense horizontally; into the strata of spiritual elements and influences that could sometimes exist in the same country, or even in the same man. Putting the Church apart for the moment, I should be disposed to divide the natural religion of the mass of mankind under such headings as these: God; the Gods; the Demons; the Philosophers. I believe some such classification will help us to sort out the spiritual experiences of men much more successfully than the conventional business of comparing religions; and that many famous figures will naturally fall into their place in this way who are only forced into their place in the other. As I shall make use of these titles or terms more than once in narrative and allusion, it will be well to define at this stage for what I mean them to stand. And I will begin with the first, the simplest and the most sublime. . . .

In considering the elements of pagan humanity, we must begin by an attempt to describe the indescribable. Many get over the difficulty of describing it by the expedient of denying it, or at least ignoring it; but the whole point of it is that it was something that was never quite eliminated even when it was ignored. They are obsessed by their evolutionary monomania that every great thing grows from a seed, or something smaller than itself. They seem to forget that every seed comes from a tree, or something larger than itself. Now there is very good ground for guessing that religion did not originally come from some detail that was forgotten, because it was too small to be traced. Much more probably it was an idea that was abandoned because it was too large to be managed. . . .

. . . Whatever else there was, there was never as such thing as the Evolution of the Idea of God. The idea was concealed, was avoided, was almost forgotten, was even explained away; but it was never evolved.

There are not a few indications of this change in other places. It is implied, for instance, in the fact that even polytheism seems often the combination of several monotheisms. A god will gain only a minor seat on Mount Olympus, when he had owned earth and heaven and all the stars while he lived in his own little valley. Like many a small nation melting in a great empire, he gives up local universality only to come under universal limitation. The very name of Pan suggests that he became a god of the wood when he had been a god of the world. The very name of Jupiter is almost a pagan translation of the words "Our Father which art in heaven." As with the Great Father symbolized by the sky, so with the Great Mother whom we still call Mother Earth. Demeter and Ceres and Cybele often seem to be almost capable of taking over the whole business of godhood, so that men should need no other gods. It seems reasonably probable that a good many men did have no other gods but one of these, worshipped as the author of all.

. . . There is the idea of God in the very notion that there were gods before the gods. There is an idea of greater simplicity in all the allusions to that more ancient order. The suggestion is supported by the process of propagation we see in historic times. Gods and demigods and heroes breed like herrings before our very eyes and suggest of themselves that the family may have had one founder; mythology grows more and more complicated, and the very complication suggests that at the beginning it was more simple. Even on the external evidence, of the sort called scientific, there is therefore a very good case for the suggestion that man began with monotheism before it developed or degenerated into polytheism. But I am concerned rather with an internal than an external truth; and, as I have already said, the internal truth is almost indescribable. We have to speak of something of which it is the whole point that people did not speak of it; we have not merely to translate from a strange tongue or speech, but from a strange silence.

I suspect an immense implication behind all polytheism and paganism. I suspect we have only a hint of it here and there in these savage creeds or Greek origins. It is not exactly what we mean by the presence of God; in a sense it might more truly be called the absence of God. But absence does not mean non-existence; and a man drinking the toast of absent friends does not mean that from his life all friendship is absent. It is a void but it is not a negation; it is something as positive as an empty chair. It would be an exaggeration to say that the pagan saw higher than Olympus an empty throne. It would be nearer the truth to take the gigantic imagery of the Old Testament, in which the prophet saw God from behind; it was as if some immeasurable presence had turned its back on the world. Yet the meaning will again be missed, if it is supposed to be anything so conscious and vivid as the monotheism of Moses and his people. I do not mean that the pagan peoples were in the least overpowered by this idea merely because it is overpowering. On the contrary, it was so large that they all carried it lightly, as we all carry the load of the sky. Gazing at some detail like a bird or a cloud, we can all ignore its awful blue background; we can neglect the sky; and precisely because it bears down upon us with an annihilating force it is felt as nothing. A thing of this kind can only be an impressing and a rather subtle impression; but to me it is a very strong impression made by pagan literature and religion. I repeat that in our special sacramental sense there is, of course, the absence of the presence of God. But there is in a very real sense the presence of the absence of God. We feel it in the unfathomable sadness of pagan poetry; for I doubt if there was ever in all the marvelous manhood of antiquity a man who was happy as St. Francis was happy. We feel it in the legend of a Golden Age and again in the vague implication that the gods themselves are ultimately related to something else, even when that Unknown God has faded into a Fate. Above all we feel it in those immortal moments when the pagan literature seems to return to a more innocent antiquity and speak with a more direct voice, so that no word is worthy of it except our own monotheistic monosyllable. We cannot say anything but "God" in a sentence like that of Socrates bidding farewell to his judges: "I go to die and you remain to live; and God alone knows which of us goes the better way." We can use no other word even for the best moments of Marcus Aurelius: "Can they say dear city of Cecrops, and canst thou not say dear city of God?" We can use no other word in that mighty line in which Virgil spoke to all who suffer with the veritable cry of a Christian before Christ: "O you that have borne things more terrible, to this also God shall give an end."

In short, there is a feeling that there is something higher than the gods; but because it is higher it is also further away. Not yet could even Virgil have read the riddle and the paradox of that other divinity, who is both higher and nearer. For them what was truly divine was very distant, so distant that they dismissed it more and more from their minds. It had less and less to do

with the mere mythology. . . . Yet even in this there was
a sort of tacit admission of its intangible purity, when
we consider what most of the mythologies like. As the
Jews would not degrade it by images, so the Greeks
did not degrade it even by imaginations. When the
gods were more and more remembered only by pranks
and profligacies, it was relatively a movement of reverence. It was an act of piety to forget God. In other
words, there is something in the whole tone of the time
suggesting that men had accepted a lower level, and
still were half conscious that it was a lower level. It is
hard to find words for these things; yet the one really
just word stands ready. These men were conscious of
the Fall if they were conscious of nothing else; and the
same is true of an heathen humanity. Those who have
fallen may remember the fall, even when they forget
the height. Some such tantalizing blank or break in
memory is at the back of all pagan sentiment. There
is such a thing as the momentary power to remember
that we forget. And the most ignorant of humanity
know by the very look of earth that they have forgotten
heaven. . . .

S

Suicidal Thinking

The phrases of the street are not only forcible but subtle: for a figure of speech can often get into a crack too small for a definition. Phrases like "put out" or "off color" might have been coined by Mr. Henry James in an agony of verbal precision. And there is no more subtle truth than that of the everyday phrase about a man having "his heart in the right place." It involves the idea of normal proportion; not only does a certain function exist, but it is rightly related to other functions. Indeed, the negation of this phrase would describe with peculiar accuracy the somewhat morbid mercy and perverse tenderness of the most representative moderns. If, for instance, I had to describe with fairness the character of Mr. Bernard Shaw, I could not express myself more exactly than by saying that he has a heroically large and generous heart; but not a heart in the right place. And this is so of the typical society of our time.

The modern world is not evil; in some ways the modern world is far too good. It is full of wild and wasted virtues. When a religious scheme is shattered (as Christianity was shattered at the Reformation), it is not merely the vices that are let loose. The vices are, indeed, let loose, and they wander and do damage. But the virtues are let loose also; and the virtues wander more wildly, and the virtues do more terrible damage. The modern world is full of the old Christian virtues gone mad. The virtues have gone mad because they have been isolated from each other and are wandering alone. Thus some scientists care for truth; and their truth is pitiless. Thus some humanitarians only care for pity; and their pity (I am sorry to say) is often untruthful. For example . . . take the acrid realist, who has deliberately killed in himself all human pleasure in happy tales or in the healing of the heart. Torquemada [fifteenth century leader of the Spanish Inquisition] tortured people physically for the sake of moral truth. Zola tortured people morally for the sake of physical truth. But in Torquemada's time there was at least a system that could to some extent make righteousness and peace kiss each other. Now they do not even bow. But a much stronger case than these two of truth and pity can be found in the remarkable case of the dislocation of humility.

It is only with one aspect of humility that we are here concerned. Humility was largely meant as a restraint upon the arrogance and infinity of the appetite of man. He was always out-stripping his mercies with his own newly invented needs. His very power of enjoyment destroyed half his joys. By asking for pleasure, he lost the chief pleasure; for the chief pleasure is surprise. Hence it became evident that if a man would make his world large, he must be always making himself small. Even the haughty visions, the tall cities, and the toppling pinnacles are the creations of humility. Giants that tread down forests like grass are the creations of humility. Towers that vanish upwards above the loneliest star are the creations of humility.

For towers are not tall unless we look up at them; and giants are not giants unless they are larger than we. All this gigantesque imagination, which is, perhaps, the mightiest of the pleasures of man, is at bottom entirely humble. It is impossible without humility to enjoy anything—even pride.

But what we suffer from today is humility in the wrong place. Modesty has moved from the organ of ambition. Modesty has settled upon the organ of conviction; where it was never meant to be. A man was meant to be doubtful about himself, but undoubting about the truth; this has been exactly reversed. Nowadays the part of a man that a man does assert is exactly the part he ought not to assert—himself. The part he doubts is exactly the part he ought not to doubt—the Divine Reason. Huxley preached a humility content to learn from Nature. But the new skeptic is so humble that he doubts if he can even learn. Thus we should be wrong if we had said hastily that there is no humility typical of our time. The truth is that there is a real humility typical of our time; but it so happens that it is practically a more poisonous humility than the wildest prostrations of the ascetic. The old humility was a spur that prevented a man from stopping; not a nail in his boot that prevented him from going on. For the old humility made a man doubtful about his efforts, which might make him work harder. But the new humility makes a man doubtful about his aims, which will make him stop working altogether.

At any street corner we may meet a man who utters the frantic and blasphemous statement that he may be wrong. Every day one comes across somebody who says that of course his view may not be the right one. Of course his view must be the right one, or it is

not his view. We are on the road to producing a race
of men too mentally modest to believe in the multipli-
cation table. We are in danger of seeing philosophers
who doubt the law of gravity as being a mere fancy of
their own. Scoffers of old time were too proud to be
convinced; but these are too humble to be convinced.
The meek do inherit the earth; but the modern sceptics are too meek even to claim their inheritance. It is
exactly this intellectual helplessness which is our second problem.

   . . . The sages, it is often said, can see no answer
to the riddle of religion. But the trouble with our sages
is not that they cannot see the answer; it is that they
cannot even see the riddle. They are like children so
stupid as to notice nothing paradoxical in the playful
assertion that a door is not a door. The modern latitudi-
narians speak, for instance, about authority in religion
not only as if there were no reason in it, but as if there
had never been any reason for it. Apart from seeing its
philosophical basis, they cannot even see its historical
cause. Religious authority has often, doubtless, been
oppressive or unreasonable; just as every legal system
(and especially our present one) has been callous and
full of a cruel apathy. It is rational to attack the police;
nay, it is glorious. But the modern critics of religious
authority are like men who should attack the police
without ever having heard of burglars. For there is a
great and possible peril to the human mind: a peril as
practical as burglary. Against it religious authority was
reared, rightly or wrongly, as a barrier. And against it
something certainly must be reared as a barrier, if our
race is to avoid ruin.

   That peril is that the human intellect is free to
destroy itself. Just as one generation could prevent

the very existence of the next generation, by all entering a monastery or jumping into the sea, so one set of
thinkers can in some degree prevent further thinking
by teaching the next generation that there is no validity
in any human thought. It is idle to talk always of the
alternative of reason and faith. Reason is itself a matter
of faith. It is an act of faith to assert that our thoughts
have any relation to reality at all. If you are merely
a sceptic, you must sooner or later ask yourself the
question, "Why should anything go right; even obser-
vation and deduction? Why should not good logic be
as misleading as bad logic? They are both movements
in the brain of a bewildered ape?" The young sceptic
says, "I have a right to think for myself." But the old
sceptic, the complete sceptic, says, "I have no right to
think for myself. I have no right to think at all."

There is a thought that stops thought. That is the
only thought that ought to be stopped. . . . The creeds
and the crusades, the hierarchies and the horrible per-
secutions were not organized, as is ignorantly said, for
the suppression of reason. They were organized for the
difficult defense of reason. Man, by a blind instinct,
knew that if once things were wildly questioned, reason could be questioned first. The authority of priests
to absolve, the authority of popes to define the authority, even of inquisitors to terrify: these were all only
dark defenses erected round one central authority,
more undemonstrable, more supernatural than all–
the authority of a man to think. We know now that
this is so; we have no excuse for not knowing it. For we
can hear skepticism crashing through the old ring of
authorities, and at the same moment we can see reason
swaying upon her throne. In so far as religion is gone,
reason is going. For they are both of the same primary

and authoritative kind. They are both methods of proof which cannot themselves be proved. And in the act of destroying the idea of Divine authority we have largely destroyed the idea of that human authority by which we do a long-division sum. With a long and sustained tug we have attempted to pull the miter off pontifical man; and his head has come off with it.

. . . This bald summary of the thought-destroying forces of our time would not be complete without some reference to pragmatism; for though I have here used and should everywhere defend the pragmatist method as a preliminary guide to truth, there is an extreme application of it which involves the absence of all truth whatever. My meaning can be put shortly thus. I agree with the pragmatists that apparent objective truth is not the whole matter; that there is an authoritative need to believe the things that are necessary to the human mind. But I say that one of those necessities precisely is a belief in objective truth. The pragmatist tells a man to think what he must think and never mind the Absolute. But precisely one of the things that he must think is the Absolute. This philosophy, indeed, is a kind of verbal paradox. Pragmatism is a matter of human needs; and one of the first of human needs is to be something more than a pragmatist. Extreme pragmatism is just as inhuman as the determinism it so powerfully attacks. The determinist (who, to do him justice, does not pretend to be a human being) makes nonsense of the human sense of actual choice. The pragmatist, who professes to be especially human, makes nonsense of the human sense of actual fact.

To sum up our contention so far, we may say that the most characteristic current philosophies have not only a touch of mania, but a touch of suicidal mania.

The mere questioner has knocked his head against the limits of human thought; and cracked it. This is what makes so futile the warnings of the orthodox and the boasts of the advanced about the dangerous boyhood of free thought. What we are looking at is not the boyhood of free thought; it is the old age and ultimate dissolution of free thought. It is vain for bishops and pious bigwigs to discuss what dreadful things will happen if wild skepticism runs its course. It has run its course. It is vain for eloquent atheists to talk of the great truths that will be revealed if once we see free thought begin. We have seen it end. It has no more questions to ask; it has questioned itself. You cannot call up any wilder vision than a city in which men ask themselves if they have any selves. You cannot fancy a more skeptical world than that in which men doubt if there is a world. . . .

. . . Here I end (thank God). . . . By the accident of my present detachment, I can see the inevitable smash of the philosophies of Schopenhauer and Tolstoy, Nietzsche and Shaw, as clearly as an inevitable railway smash could be seen from a balloon. They are all on the road to the emptiness of the asylum. For madness may be defined as using mental activity so as to reach mental helplessness; and they have nearly reached it. He who thinks he is made of glass, thinks to the destruction of thought; for glass cannot think. So he who wills to reject nothing, wills the destruction of will; for will is not only the choice of something, but the rejection of almost everything. And as I turn and tumble over the clever, wonderful, tiresome, and useless modern books, the title of one of them rivets my eye. It is called *Jeanne d'Arc*, by Anatole France. I have only glanced at it, but a glance was enough to remind me of Renan's *Vie de Jesus*. It has the same strange method of the reverent skeptic. It discredits supernatural stories that have some foundation, simply by telling natural stories that have no foundation. Because we cannot believe in what a saint did, we are to pretend that we know exactly what he felt. But I do not mention either book in order to criticize it, but because the accidental combination of the names called up two startling images of sanity which blasted all the books before me. Joan of Arc was not stuck at the crossroads, either by rejecting all the paths like Tolstoy, or by accepting them all like Nietzsche. She chose a path, and went down it like a thunderbolt. Yet Joan, when I came to think of her, had in her all that was true either in Tolstoy or Nietzsche, all that was even tolerable in either of them. I thought of all that is noble in Tolstoy, the pleasure in plain things, especially in plain pity, the actualities of the earth, the reverence for the poor, the dignity of the bowed back. Joan of Arc had all that and with this great addition, that she endured poverty as well as admiring it; whereas Tolstoy is only a typical aristocrat trying to find out its secret. And then I thought of all that was brave and proud and pathetic in poor Nietzsche, and his mutiny against the emptiness and timidity of our time. I thought of his cry for the ecstatic equilibrium of danger, his hunger for the rush of great horses, his cry to arms. Well, Joan of Arc had all that, and again with this difference, that she did not praise fighting, but fought. We know that she was not afraid of an army, while Nietzsche, for all we know, was afraid of a cow. Tolstoy only praised the peasant; she was the peasant. Nietzsche only praised the warrior; she was the warrior. She beat them both at their own antagonistic ideals; she was more gentle than the one, more violent than the other. Yet she was a perfectly practical person who did something, while they are wild speculators who do nothing. It was impossible that the thought should not cross my mind that she and her faith had perhaps some secret of moral unity and utility that has been lost. And with that thought came a larger one, and the colossal figure of her Master had also crossed the theatre of my thoughts. The same modern difficulty which darkened the subject-matter of Anatole France also darkened that of Ernest Renan. Renan also divided his hero's pity from his hero's pugnacity. Renan even represented the righteous anger at Jerusalem as a mere nervous breakdown after the idyllic expectations of Galilee. As if there were any inconsistency between having a love for humanity and having a hatred for inhumanity! Altruists, with thin, weak voices, denounce Christ as an egoist. Egoists (with even thinner and weaker voices) denounce Him as an altruist. In our present atmosphere such cavils are comprehensible enough. The love of a hero is more terrible than the hatred of a tyrant. The hatred of a hero is more generous than the love of a philanthropist. There is a huge and heroic sanity of which moderns can only collect the fragments. There is a giant of whom we see only the lopped arms and legs walking about. They have torn the soul of Christ into silly strips, labelled egoism and altruism, and they are equally puzzled by His insane magnificence and His insane meekness. They have parted His garments among them, and for His vesture they have cast lots; though the coat was without seam woven from the top throughout.

T

St. Thomas Aquinas

I do not know for certain why St. Thomas was called the Angelic Doctor: whether it was that he had an angelic temper, or the intellectuality of an Angel; or whether there was a later legend that he concentrated on Angels—especially on the points of needles. If so, I do not quite understand how this idea arose; history has many examples of an irritating habit of labeling somebody in connection with something, as if he never did anything else. Who was it who began the inane habit of referring to Dr. Johnson as "our lexicographer"; as if he never did anything but write a dictionary? Why do most people insist on meeting the large and far-reaching mind of Pascal at its very narrowest point: the point at which it was sharpened into a spike by the spite of the Jansenists against the Jesuits? It is just possible, for all I know, that this labeling of Aquinas as a specialist was an obscure depreciation of him as a universalist. For that is a very common trick for the belittling of literary or scientific men. St. Thomas must have made a certain number of enemies, though he hardly ever treated them as enemies. Unfortunately, good temper is sometimes more irritating than bad temper. And he had, after all, done a great deal of damage, as many medieval men would have thought; and, what is more curious, a great deal of damage to both sides. He had been a revolutionist against Augustine and a traditionalist against Averroes [twelfth-century Islamic philosopher]. He might appear to some to have tried to wreck that ancient beauty of the city of God, which bore some resemblance to the Republic of Plato. He might appear to others to have inflicted a blow on the advancing and leveling forces of Islam, as dramatic as that of Godfrey storming Jerusalem [in the First Crusade]. It is possible that these enemies, by wax of damning with faint praise, talked about his very respectable little work on Angels: as a man might say that Darwin was really reliable when writing on coral-insects; or that some of Milton's Latin poems were very creditable indeed. But this is only a conjecture, and many other conjectures are possible. And I am disposed to think that St. Thomas really was rather especially interested in the nature of Angels, for the same reason that made him even more interested in the nature of Men. It was a part of that strong personal interest in things subordinate and semi-dependent, which runs through his whole system: a hierarchy of higher and lower liberties. He was interested in the problem of the Angel, as he was interested in the problem of the Man, because it was a problem; and especially because it was a problem of an intermediate creature. I do not pretend to deal here with this mysterious quality, as he conceives it to exist in that inscrutable intellectual being, who is less than God but more than Man. But it was this quality of a link in the chain, or a rung in the ladder, which mainly concerned the theologian, in developing his own particular theory of degrees. Above all, it is this which chiefly moves him, when he finds so fascinating the central mystery of

Man. And for him the point is always that Man is not a balloon going up into the sky nor a mole burrowing merely in the earth; but rather a thing like a tree, whose roots are fed from the earth, while its highest branches seem to rise almost to the stars.

I have pointed out that mere modern free-thought has left everything in a fog, including itself. The assertion that thought is free led first to the denial that will is free; but even about that there was no real determination among the Determinists. In practice, they told men that they must treat their will as free though it was not free. . . . In other words, the nineteenth century left everything in chaos: and the importance of Thomism to the twentieth century is that it may give us back a cosmos. We can give here only the rudest sketch of how Aquinas, like the Agnostics, beginning in the cosmic cellars, yet climbed to the cosmic towers.

Without pretending to span within such limits the essential Thomist idea, I may be allowed to throw out a sort of rough version of the fundamental question, which I think I have known myself, consciously or unconsciously since my childhood. When a child looks out of the nursery window and sees anything, say the green lawn of the garden, what does he actually know; or does he know anything? There are all sorts of nursery games of negative philosophy played round this question. A brilliant Victorian scientist delighted in declaring that the child does not see any grass at all; but only a sort of green mist reflected in a tiny mirror of the human eye. This piece of rationalism has always struck me as almost insanely irrational. If he is not sure of the existence of the grass, which he sees through the glass of a window, how on earth can he be sure of the existence of the retina, which he sees through the glass of a microscope? If sight deceives, why can it not go on deceiving? Men of another school answer that grass is a mere green impression on the mind and that he can be sure of nothing except the mind. They declare that he can only be conscious of his own consciousness; which happens to be the one thing that we know the child is not conscious of at all. In that sense, it would be far truer to say that there is grass and no child, than to say that there is a conscious child but no grass. St. Thomas Aquinas, suddenly intervening in this nursery quarrel, says emphatically that the child is aware of *Ens* [Latin, "Being"]. Long before he knows that grass is grass, or self is self, he knows that something is something. Perhaps it would be best to say very emphatically (with a blow on the table), "There is an Is." That is as much monkish credulity as St. Thomas asks of us at the start. Very few unbelievers start by asking us to believe so little. And yet, upon this sharp pin-point of reality, he rears by long logical processes that have never really been successfully overthrown, the whole cosmic system of Christendom.

Thus, Aquinas insists very profoundly but very practically, that there instantly enters, with this idea of affirmation the idea of contradiction. It is instantly apparent, even to the child, that there cannot be both affirmation and contradiction. Whatever you call the thing he sees, a moon or a mirage or a sensation or a state of consciousness, when he sees it, he knows it is not true that he does not see it. Or whatever you call what he is supposed to be doing, seeing or dreaming or being conscious of an impression, he knows that if he is doing it, it is a lie to say he is not doing it. Therefore there has already entered something beyond even the first fact of being; there follows it like its shadow the first fundamental creed or commandment, that a thing cannot be and not be. Henceforth, in common or popular language, there is a false and true. I say in popular language, because Aquinas is nowhere more subtle than in pointing out that being is not strictly the same as truth; seeing truth must mean the appreciation of being by some mind capable of appreciating it. But in a general sense there has entered that primeval world of pure actuality, the division and dilemma that brings the ultimate sort of war into the world; the everlasting duel between Yes and No. This is the dilemma that many sceptics have darkened the universe and dissolved the mind solely in order to escape. They are those who maintain that there is something that is both Yes and No. I do not know whether they pronounce it Yo.

The next step following on this acceptance of actuality or certainty, or whatever we call it in popular language, is much more difficult to explain in that language. But it represents exactly the point at which nearly all other systems go wrong, and in taking the third step abandon the first. Aquinas has affirmed that our first sense of fact is a fact; and he cannot go back on it without falsehood. But when we come to look at the fact or facts, as we know them, we observe that they have a rather queer character; which has made many moderns grow strangely and restlessly skeptical about them. For instance, they are largely in a state of change, from being one thing to being another; or their qualities are relative to other things; or they appear to move incessantly; or they appear to vanish entirely. At this point, as I say, many sages lose hold of the first principle of reality, which they would concede at first; and fall back on saying that there is nothing except change;

or nothing except comparison; or nothing except flux; or in effect that there is nothing at all. Aquinas turns the whole argument the other way, keeping in line with his first realization of reality. There is no doubt about the being of being, even if it does sometimes look like becoming; that is because what we see is not the fullness of being; or (to continue a sort of colloquial slang) we never see being being as much as it can. Ice is melted into cold water and cold water is heated into hot water; it cannot be all three at once. But this does not make water unreal or even relative; it only means that its being is limited to being one thing at a time. But the fullness of being is everything that it can be; and without it the lesser or approximate forms of being cannot be explained as anything; unless they are explained away as nothing.

This crude outline can only at the best be historical rather than philosophical. It is impossible to compress into it the metaphysical proofs of such an idea; especially in the medieval metaphysical language. But this distinction in philosophy is tremendous as a turning point in history. Most thinkers, on realizing the apparent mutability of being, have really forgotten their own realization of the being, and believed only in the mutability. They cannot even say that a thing changes into another thing; for them there is no instant in the process at which it is a thing at all. It is only a change. It would be more logical to call it nothing changing into nothing, than to say (on these principles) that there ever was or will be a moment when the thing is itself. St. Thomas maintains that the ordinary thing at any moment is something; but it is not everything that it could be. There is a fullness of being, in which it could be everything that it can be. Thus, while most sages come at last to nothing but naked change, he comes to the ultimate thing that is unchangeable, because it is all the other things at once. While they describe a change which is really a change in nothing, he describes a changelessness which includes the changes of everything. Things change because they are not complete; but their reality can only be explained as part of something that is complete. It is God.

Historically, at least, it was round this sharp and crooked corner that all the sophists have followed each other while the great Schoolman [St. Thomas, the pre-eminent "Schoolman," or Scholastic theologian] went up the high road of experience and expansion; to the beholding of cities, to the building of cities. They all failed at this early stage because, in the words of the old game, they took away the number they first thought of. The recognition of something, of a thing or things, is the first act of the intellect. But because the examination of a thing shows it is not a fixed or final thing, they inferred that there is nothing fixed or final. Thus, in various ways, they all began to see a thing as something thinner than a thing; a wave; a weakness; an abstract instability. St. Thomas, to use the same rude figure, saw a thing that was thicker than a thing; that was even more solid than the solid but secondary facts he had started by admitting as facts. Since we know them to be real, any elusive or bewildering element in their reality cannot really be unreality; and must be merely their relation to the real reality. A hundred human philosophies, ranging over the earth from Nominalism to Nirvana and Maya, from formless evolution to mindless quietism, all come from this first break in the Thomist chain; the notion that, because what we see does not satisfy us or explain itself, it is not even what we see. That cosmos is a contradiction in terms and strangles itself; but Thomism cuts itself free. The defect we see, in what is, is simply that it is not all that is. God is more actual even than Man; more actual even than Matter; for God with all His powers at every instant is immortally in action.

A cosmic comedy of a very curious sort occurred recently; involving the views of very brilliant men, such as Mr. Bernard Shaw and the Dean of St. Paul's. Briefly, freethinkers of many sorts had often said they had no need of a Creation, because the cosmos had always existed and always would exist. Mr. Bernard Shaw said he had become an atheist because the universe had gone on making itself from the beginning or without a beginning; Dean Inge later displayed consternation at the very idea that the universe could have an end. Most modern Christians, living by tradition where medieval Christians could live by logic or reason, vaguely felt that it was a dreadful idea to deprive them of the Day of Judgment. Most modern agnostics (who are delighted to have their ideas called dreadful) cried out all the more, with one accord, that the self-producing, self-existent, truly scientific universe had never needed to have a beginning and could not come to an end. At this very instant, quite suddenly, like the look-out man on a ship who shouts a warning about a rock, the real man of science, the expert who was examining the facts, announced in a loud voice that the universe was coming to an end. He had not been listening, of course, to the talk of the amateurs; he had been actually examining the texture of matter; and he said it was disintegrating: the world was apparently blowing itself up by a gradual explosion called energy; the whole business would certainly have an end and had presumably had a beginning. This was very shocking indeed; not to the orthodox, but rather especially to the unorthodox; who are rather more easily shocked. Dean Inge, who had been lecturing the orthodox for years on their stern duty of accepting all scientific discoveries, positively wailed aloud over this truly tactless scientific discovery, and practically implored the scientific discoverers to go away and discover something different. It seems almost incredible; but it is a fact that he asked what God would have to amuse Him, if the universe ceased. That is a measure of how much the modern mind needs Thomas Aquinas. But even without Aquinas, I can hardly conceive any educated man, let alone such a learned man, believing in God at all without assuming that God contains in Himself every perfection including eternal joy; and does not require the solar system to entertain him like a circus.

To step out of these presumptions, prejudices and private disappointments, into the world of St. Thomas, is like escaping from a scuffle in a dark room into the broad daylight. St. Thomas says, quite straightforwardly, that he himself believes this world has a beginning and end; because such seems to be the teaching of the Church; the validity of which mystical message to mankind he defends elsewhere with dozens of quite different arguments. Anyhow, the Church said the world would end; and apparently the Church was right; always supposing (as we are always supposed to suppose) that the latest men of science are right. But Aquinas says he sees no particular reason, in reason, why this world should not be a world without end; or even without beginning. And he is quite certain that, if it were entirely without end or beginning, there would still be exactly the same logical need of a Creator. Anybody who does not see that, he gently implies, does not really understand what is meant by a Creator.

For what St. Thomas means is not a medieval picture of an old king; but this second step in the great argument about *Ens* or Being; the second point which is so desperately difficult to put correctly in popular language. That is why I have introduced it here in the particular form of the argument that there must be a Creator even if there is no Day of Creation. Looking at Being as it is now, as the baby looks at the grass, we see a second thing about it; in quite popular language, it looks secondary and dependent. Existence exists; but it is not sufficiently self-existent; and would never become so merely by going on existing. The same primary sense which tells us it is Being, tells us that it is not perfect Being; not merely imperfect in the popular controversial sense of containing sin or sorrow; but imperfect as Being; less actual than the actuality it implies. For instance, its Being is often only Becoming; beginning to Be or ceasing to Be; it implies a more constant or complete thing of which it gives in itself no example. That is the meaning of that basic medieval phrase, "Everything that is moving is moved by another"; which, in the clear subtlety of St. Thomas, means inexpressibly more than the mere Deistic "somebody wound up the clock" with which it is probably often confounded. Anyone who thinks deeply will see that motion has about it an essential incompleteness, which approximates to something more complete.

The actual argument is rather technical; and concerns the fact that potentiality does not explain itself; moreover, in any case, unfolding must be of something folded. Suffice it to say that the mere modern evolutionists, who would ignore the argument do not do so because they have discovered any flaw in the argument; for they have never discovered the argument itself. They do so because they are too shallow to see the flaw in their own argument for the weakness of their thesis is covered by fashionable phraseology, as the strength of the old thesis is covered by old-fashioned phraseology. But for those who really think, there is always something really unthinkable about the whole evolutionary cosmos, as they conceive it; because it is something coming out of nothing; an ever-increasing flood of water pouring out of an empty jug. Those who can simply accept that, without even seeing the difficulty, are not likely to go so deep as Aquinas and see the solution of his difficulty. In a word, the world does not explain itself, and cannot do so merely by continuing to expand itself. But anyhow it is absurd for the Evolutionist to complain that it is unthinkable for an admittedly unthinkable God to make everything out of nothing and then pretend that it is more thinkable that nothing should turn itself into everything.

. . . But we do not need even St. Thomas, we do not need anything but our own common sense, to tell us that if there has been from the beginning anything that can possibly be called a Purpose, it must reside in something that has the essential elements of a Person. There cannot be an intention hovering in the air all by itself, any more than a memory that nobody remembers or a joke that nobody has made. The only chance for those supporting such suggestions is to take refuge in blank and bottomless irrationality; and even then it is impossible to prove that anybody has any right to be unreasonable, if St. Thomas has no right to be reasonable.

In a sketch that aims only at the baldest simplification, this does seem to me the simplest truth about St. Thomas the philosopher. He is one, so to speak, who is faithful to his first love; and it is love at first sight. I mean that he immediately recognized a real quality in things; and afterwards resisted all the disintegrating doubts arising from the nature of those things. That is why I emphasize . . . the fact that there is a sort of purely Christian humility and fidelity underlying his philosophic realism. St. Thomas could as truly say, of having seen merely a stick or a stone, what St. Paul said of having seen the rending of the secret heavens, "I was not disobedient to the heavenly vision." For though the stick or the stone is an earthly vision, it is through them that St. Thomas finds his way to heaven; and the point is that he is obedient to the vision; he does not go back on it. Nearly all the other sages who have led or misled mankind do, on one excuse or another, go back on it. They dissolve the stick or the stone in chemical solutions of skepticism; either in the medium of mere time and change; or in the difficulties of classification of unique units; or in the difficulty of recognizing variety while admitting unity. The first of these three is called debate about flux or formless transition; the second is the debate about Nominalism and Realism, or the existence of general ideas; the third is called the ancient metaphysical riddle of the One and the Many. But they can all be reduced under a rough image to this same statement about St. Thomas. He is still true to the first truth and refusing the first treason. He will not deny what he has seen, though it be a secondary and diverse reality. He will not take away the numbers he

first thought of, though there may be quite a number
of them.

. . . The first flash of fact shows us a world of really
strange things not merely strange to us, but strange to
each other. The separate things need have nothing in
common except Being. Everything is Being; but it is not
true that everything is Unity. It is here, as I have said,
that St. Thomas does definitely one might say defiantly, part company with the Pantheist and Monist. All
things are; but among the things that are is the thing
called difference, quite as much as the thing called similarity. And here again we begin to be bound again to
the Lord, not only by the universality of grass, but by
the incompatibility of grass and gravel. For this world
of different and varied beings is especially the world of
the Christian Creator; the world of created things, like
things made by an artist; as compared with the world
that is only one thing, with a sort of shimmering and
shifting veil of misleading change; which is the conception of so many of the ancient religions of Asia and
the modern sophistries of Germany. In the face of these,
St. Thomas still stands stubborn in the same obstinate
objective fidelity. He has seen grass and gravel; and he
is not disobedient to the heavenly vision.

To sum up; the reality of things, the mutability of
things, the diversity of things, and all other such things
that can be attributed to things, is followed carefully by
the medieval philosopher, without losing touch with
the original point of the reality. . . . He is a realist in a
rather curious sense of his own, which is a third thing,
distinct from the almost contrary medieval and modern meanings of the word. Even the doubts and difficulties about reality have driven him to believe in more
reality rather than less. The deceitfulness of things

which has had so sad an effect on so many sages, has
almost a contrary effect on this sage. If things deceive
us, it is by being more real than they seem. As ends
in themselves they always deceive us; but as things
tending to a greater end, they are even more real than
we think them. If they seem to have a relative unreality
(so to speak) it is because they are potential and not
actual; they are unfulfilled, like packets of seeds or
boxes of fireworks. They have it in them to be more real
than they are. And there is an upper world of what the
Schoolman called Fruition, or Fulfillment, in which all
this relative relativity becomes actuality; in which the
trees burst into flower or the rockets into flame.

U

Upon This Rock

To a Roman Catholic the Roman Catholic Church is
simply the Christian religion; the gift of Christ to St.
Peter and his successors of a right to answer at all times
all questions about what it really is; a thing surrounded
at the edge of its own wide domain by various severed
fragments of its own substance; consisting of people
who for different reasons deny that right to affirm what
it really is, and who therefore differ among themselves,
indefinitely and increasingly, about what it really is. It
may be added that they differ not only about the nature
of the ideal Christianity that ought to be substituted,
but even about the nature of the Roman Catholicism
that is to be defied. To some it is Antichrist; to some it
is one branch of the Church of Christ, having authority
in certain provinces but not in England or Russia; to
some it is a corrupt perversion of Truth from which
religion was rescued; to others a necessary historic
phase through which religion had to pass; and so on.
But it may be noted by the curious that though there is
so much difference in the reasons given, there is something common to most of the emotions felt. The reactions to Rome are all reactions to something odd. It is
a thousand things, but all things with a sort of thrill in
them; a mystery, a *bete noire*, a strange survival, a public

scandal, a private embarrassment, an open secret, a
tactless topic, a sly joke, a last refuge or a leap in the
dark: everything except anything that is like anything
else.

To a Roman Catholic there is no particular difference between those parts of the religion which
Protestants and others accept and those parts which
they reject. The dogmas have, of course, their intrinsic theological proportions; but in his feeling they are
all one thing. The Mass is as Christian as the Gospel.
The Gospel is as Catholic as the Mass. This, I fancy, is
the fact which the Protestant world has found it most
difficult to understand and about which some of the
most unfortunate forms of ill-feeling have appeared.
Yet it arises quite naturally from the actual history of
the Church, which has had to contend incessantly with
quite other and quite opposite heresies. She has not
only had to defeat these sects to defend these doctrines,
but to defeat other sects to defend other doctrines
including the doctrines which these sects rightly hold
so dear. It was only the Roman Catholic Church that
saved the Protestant truths. It may be right to rest on
the Bible, but there would be no Bible if the Gnostics
had proved that the Old Testament was written by the
Devil, or had littered the world with Apocryphal Gospels. It may be right to say that Jesus alone saves from
sin, but nobody would be saying it if a Pelagian movement had altered the whole notion of sin. Even the
very selection of dogmas which the reformers decided
to preserve had only been preserved for them by the
authority which they denied.

It is natural, therefore, for Catholics not to be
always thinking of the antithesis of Catholic and Protestant any more than of Catholic and Pelagian. Catholicism is used to proposals to cut down the creed to a

few clauses; but different people have wanted quite different clauses left and quite different clauses cut out. Thus a Catholic does not feel the special reverence paid to the Mother of God as any more of a controversial question than the divine honors paid to the Son of God; for he knows the latter was as much controverted by the Arians as the former by the Puritans. He does not feel the throne of St. Peter to be any more specially in dispute than the theology of St. Paul, for he knows that both have been disputed. There have been anti-popes; there have been Apocryphal Gospels; there have been sects dethroning our Lady and sects dethroning our Lord. After nearly two thousand years of this sort of thing, Catholics have come to regard Catholicism as one thing, all the parts of which are in one sense equally assailed and in another sense equally unassailable.

Now it is unfortunately impossible for a Roman Catholic to state the principle without its sounding provocative and, what is much worse, superior; but unless he does state it, he does not state Roman Catholicism. Having stated it, however, in its dogmatic and defiant form, as it is his duty to do, he may afterwards suggest something of why the system seems, to those inside it, to be not so much a system as a home, and even a holiday. Thus it certainly does not mean being superior in the sense of supercilious; for in this system alone, only the saint is superior because he feels he is inferior. It does not say that all heretics are lost, for it does say that there is a common conscience by which they may be saved. But it does definitely say that he who knows the whole truth sins in accepting half the truth. Thus the Church is not a movement, like all those which have filled the world since the sixteenth century; that is, since the breakdown of the collective attempt of all Christendom to state the whole truth. It is not the movement of something trying to find its balance; it is the balance. But the point here is that even those heretics, who snatched at half-truths, seldom snatched at the same half. The original Protestants insisted on Hell without Purgatory. Their modern successors generally insist on Purgatory without Hell. Their future successors may quite possibly insist on Purgatory without Heaven. It may seem a natural sequence to the worship of Progress for its own sake, and the theory that "to travel hopefully is better than to arrive." For the Catholic each of these things may be disputed in its turn, and all will remain.

Nevertheless, in making so short a summary in a world still Protestant by tradition, it will be convenient to assume that the reader is acquainted with the Christian scheme in those features which, until lately, were common to many or most Christian bodies: the Image of God, the Fall, the necessity of Redemption, the Last Judgment, and the rest; and to describe the Catholic faith (from which all these things really come) as that world sees it, by the chief features that appear distinctive because they are disputed. I will therefore say a word or two of what would still be commonly called the marks of Roman Catholicism. I shall say very little about the greatest of all, because it is admittedly a mystery and an object of faith. Catholics believe that in the Blessed Sacrament Christ is present, not merely as a thought is present in a mind, but as a person is present in a room, veiled only from the actual senses by the appearances of bread and wine. Of its historical aspect it will be enough to say that Roman Catholics are convinced that it is spoken of in this spirit at least as early as St. Ignatius, who was roughly of the next generation to that of the Gospel. The common sense of it, it seems to me, would be to say that if the words of Christ at the Last Supper were misunderstood, they were misunderstood by the twelve Apostles. But the doctrine is so tremendous and transcendental that we cannot complain if some misunderstand it as blasphemous and extravagant. Only they cannot have it both ways. They must not turn round and complain that we claim to possess Christ as a living God by a vital process, absent from the other communions that called the process impossible. They must not grumble at our talking of Christ coming back to a heretic land with the first procession bearing the Host. There must be a difference between Christ's presence in their sense and in our sense, if they are actually shocked and staggered at our sense. A Return which they are driven to call impossible we may surely be allowed to call unique.

For practical purposes in Protestant civilization it is another fact that soars most clearly into sight, towering even over Transubstantiation. It is the Papacy that makes the Papist. For him, at least, it dates from the highly dramatic words about the Rock and the Gates of Hell; it certainly appears, to say the very least, as an admitted seat of superior authority in the debates of the first Fathers and Councils; but it was not logically and literally defined until the middle of the nineteenth century. In this sense it is true that the idea grew; but we can never make anything but nonsense out of the sort of evolution that imagines something growing out of nothing. But in so far as an eternal truth can grow, in the comprehension of men, it has grown continuously with the increase of the experience of men. The general case for a tribunal to define the truth has been touched upon already. I pointed out that long before Protestants rushed in to preserve their simple Christianity, even that simple Christianity would not have been there to preserve if there had not already been a Church tribunal to preserve it. The question then becomes one of the nature of the tribunal. Even if democracy were applicable to a revelation, there could not really be a democratic tribunal which should be deciding all the time and democratic all the time. It would not be the millions of poor and humble Catholics who would rule; it would be the officials if it were not the official. It would be a Holy Synod. Now every popular instinct Catholics possess seems to them to say that rather than have merely an official order, that is, an oligarchy, it is far more human to have a monarchy, that is, a man. It is indeed remarkable that those who broke with this purely moral monarchy generally set up a material and a rather immoral monarchy. The first great schism in the East was made by men who turned from the Popes to bow down to the Caesars and the Tsars. The last great schism in the West was made by men who attributed divine right to Henry VIII, not to mention Charles I. Those who thought the papacy too despotic did not even escape despotism.

It is needless to explain, I trust, that the only despotism of the Pope consists in the fact that all Catholics believe that God will guard him from teaching falsehood to the Church on those special and rather rare occasions when he is appealed to end a controversy with a final statement of faith. His ordinary pronouncements, though naturally received with profound respect, are not infallible. His private character depends on his own free will, like anybody else's. He can commit sins like anybody else; he must confess sins like anybody else; and his having been Pope is nothing to his salvation. But the question is, given our need for such final decisions to save Christianity at great crises, what organ of the Church decides? The longer historical experience accumulates, the more profoundly thankful most Catholics are that the organ is a human being; a mind and not a type, a will and not a tradition or tone of a class. The best bishops ruling as a class would become a club, as a parliament does. They would have all of its scattered responsibility, all its mutual flattery, all its diffused and dangerous pride. But the responsibility of a Pope is so solitary and so solemn that a man would need to be a maniac not to be humbled by it.

Probably the Protestant world would count as the next outstanding feature, after the power of the priests to perform Mass and of the Popes to define doctrine, that other power of the priesthood which is expressed in the sacrament of Penance. The sacramental system is everywhere based on the idea that certain material acts are mystical acts; are events in the spiritual world. This mystical materialism does divide us from all those forms of idealism that hold all good to be inward and invisible and matter to be unworthy to express it. It is needless to note how this applies to the water of baptism, the oil of unction, and so on. But I am deliberately taking the sacrament which our world has most misunderstood; and, strangely enough, it is that one which is least material and most spiritual, consisting of spoken words expressing the most secret thoughts. Of all the sacraments it is, in the modern jargon, the most psychological. And the proof of it is that even the people who abolished it a few centuries ago found that they had to invent a new imitation of it a few years ago. They told the people to go to a new priest, often without credentials, and make confession generally without absolution, and they called it psychoanalysis. Catholicism would say that the lack of the confessional had produced a modern congestion and stagnation of secrets so morbid as to be reaching the verge of madness.

Broadly, it may be said that Roman Catholicism has had the idea, hitherto at least highly unique, of working mankind from the inside. There have been and are any number of external ethical and political systems directing men how to do right in the mass; there is no other that thus gets to grips with why such a system goes wrong with the individual. Most moderns are content to get hold of the plan of Utopia. This is rather like getting hold of the diary of the Utopian and learning the real reason why he does not always behave in a Utopian manner. But, of course, it is quite useless unless he produces his own diary of his own free will. Unless he really wishes it, there can be no sacrament; and unless he really repents, there is no absolution. For the history of this institution, it follows in its rough outline the same course as the other cases of the Mass and the Papacy. That is, it is undoubtedly present as an idea in the very earliest times; there are disputes about the proportion of that presence, and there need be no dispute at all that it grew more elaborate, more systematic, and more subtle with the process of experience. What is called Development is the unfolding of all the consequences and applications of an idea; but of something that is there, not of something that is not there. In this sense the Catholic Church is the one Christian body that has always believed in Evolution.

There is barely space to touch on two more of these things which are counted Popish specialties chiefly because they are counted Popish scandals. The first is the idea of asceticism and especially of celibacy. The second is the cult of the Blessed Virgin. Of the former it will be enough to say here that to most ordinary Roman Catholics, who are not called upon to practice special austerities, those examples are valuable not only as examples of heroism, but as very vivid evidences of the reality of religious hopes. Granted that for us the divine light is valued as a daily light, brightening our daily and normal affairs, yet it would not brighten them at all if we did not believe that the light was really divine. If we only believed that religion was useful, it would be of no use. Now nothing could better prove the light divine than that some should live on it as on a food; nothing could more clearly show religion to be real than that for some people it can be a substitute for other realities. We have no difficulty in believing that such people deal more directly with divine things than we, as in the case of those who enjoy directly a divine love instead of indirectly through a human love in marriage. And when we are criticized for this, we remember with some amusement that it was we who said that marriage was a divine sacrament when our critics said it was not.

Of the most popular, the most poetical and the most practically inspiring of all the distinctively Catholic traditions of Christianity, I will say very little here; indeed, I will say only one thing. The honor given to Mary as the Mother of God is, among a thousand other things, a very perfect example of the truth to which I have recurred more than once: that even what we may call the Protestant truths were only saved by the Catholic authority. Among these is the very necessary truth of the subordination of Mary to Christ, as being after all the subordination of the creature to the Creator. Nothing amuses Catholics more than the suggestion, in so much of the old Protestant propaganda, that they are to be freed from the superstition called Mariolatry, like people freed from the burden of daylight. All the spontaneous spirituality, as distinct from the necessary doctrinal orthodoxy, is on the side of the extension and even excess of this cult. If Catholics had been left to their private judgment, to their personal religious experience, to their sense of the essential spirit of Christ and Christianity, to any of the liberal or latitudinarian tests of truth, they would long ago have exalted our Lady to a height of superhuman supremacy and splendor that might really have imperiled the pure monotheism in the core of the creed. Over whole tracts of popular opinion she might have been a goddess more universal than Isis. It is the authority of Rome that has prevented such Catholics from indulging in such Mariolatry; the strict definition that distinguished between a perfect woman and a divine Man. But if it were a place for expression of feeling, little doubt would be left about which way all our most direct and democratic feelings drive. I have throughout this statement ignored the meaningless affectation of impartiality. It is impossible for any man to state what he believes as if he did not believe it. But I have endeavored to describe the most familiar features of this one religion in terms of logic not of rhetoric. And on this last matter of the doctrine touching the Virgin I will conclude without further speech. It is only reasonable that a creed presented by one who holds it should be stated with conviction; but anything I wrote on this last topic might be defaced with enthusiasm.

V

Queen Victoria

Anyone who possesses spiritual or political courage
has made up his mind to a prospect of immutable
mutability; but even in a "transformation" there is
something catastrophic in the removal of the back
scene. It is a truism to say of the wise and noble lady
who is gone from us that we shall always remember
her; but there is a subtler and higher compliment still
in confessing that we often forgot her. We forgot her
as we forget the sunshine, as we forget the postulates
of an argument, as we commonly forget our own
existence. Mr. Gladstone [four-time prime minister of
England] is the only figure whose loss prepared us
for such earthquakes altering the landscape. But Mr.
Gladstone seemed a fixed and stationary object in our
age for the same reason that one railway train looks
stationary from another; because he and the age of
progress were both travelling at the same impetuous
rate of speed. In the end, indeed, it was probably the
age that dropped behind. For a symbol of the Queen's
position we must rather recur to the image of a stretch
of scenery, in which she was as a mountain so huge and
familiar that its disappearance would make the landscape round our own door seem like a land of strang-
ers. She had an inspired genius for the familiarizing

virtues; her sympathy and sanity made us feel at home even in an age of revolutions. That indestructible sense of security which for good and evil is so typical of our nation, that almost scornful optimism which, in the matter of ourselves, cannot take peril or even decadence seriously, reached by far its highest and healthiest form in the sense that we were watched over by one so thoroughly English in her silence and self-control, in her shrewd trustfulness and her brilliant inaction. Over and above those sublime laws of labor and pity by which she ordered her life, there are a very large number of minor intellectual matters in which we might learn a lesson from the Queen. There is one especially which is increasingly needed in an age when moral claims become complicated and hysterical. That Queen Victoria was a model of political unselfishness is well known; it is less often remarked that few modern people have an unselfishness so completely free from morbidity, so fully capable of deciding a moral question without exaggerating its importance. No eminent person of our time has been so utterly devoid of that disease of self-assertion which is often rampant among the unselfish. She had one most rare and valuable faculty, the faculty of letting things pass—Acts of Parliament and other things. Her predecessors, whether honest men or knaves, were attacked every now and then with a nightmare of despotic responsibility; they suddenly conceived that it rested with them to save the world and the Protestant Constitution. Queen Victoria had far too much faith in the world to try to save it. She knew that Acts of Parliament, even bad Acts of Parliament, do not destroy nations. But she knew that ignorance, ill-temper, tyranny, and officiousness do destroy nations, and not upon any provocation would she set an example in these things. We fancy that this sense of proportion, this largeness and coolness of intellectual magnanimity is the one of the thousand virtues of Queen Victoria of which the near future will stand most in need. We are gaining many new mental powers, and with them new mental responsibilities. In psychology, in sociology, above all in education, we are learning to do a great many clever things. Unless we are much mistaken the next great task will be to learn not to do them. If that time comes, assuredly we cannot do better than turn once more to the memory of the great Queen who for seventy years followed through every possible tangle and distraction the fairy thread of common sense.

. . . Both royalty and religion have been accused of despising humanity, and in practice it has been too often true; but after all both the conception of the prophet and that of the king were formed by paying humanity that she stood, for the humblest, the shortest and the at random. This daring idea that a healthy human being, when thrilled by all the trumpets of a great trust, would rise to the situation, has often been tested, but never with such complete success as in the case of our dead Queen. On her was piled the crushing load of a vast and mystical tradition, and she stood up straight under it. Heralds proclaimed her as the anointed of God, and it did not seem presumptuous. Brave men died in thousands shouting her name, and it did not seem unnatural. No mere intellect, no mere worldly success could, in this age of bold inquiry, have sustained that tremendous claim; long ago we should have stricken Caesar and dethroned Napoleon. But these glories and these sacrifices did not seem too much to celebrate a hardworking human nature; they were possible because at the heart of our Empire was nothing but a defiant humility. If the Queen had stood for any novel or fantastic imperial claims, the whole would have seemed a nightmare; the whole was successful because she stood, and no one could deny the supreme compliment of selecting from it almost most indestructible of human gospels, that when all troubles and troublemongers have had their say, our work can be done till sunset, our life can be lived till death.

W

Words

Everyone has his own private and almost secret selection among the examples of the mysterious power of words, the power which a certain verbal combination has over the emotions and even the soul. It is commonplace that literature has a charm, not merely in the sense of the charm of a woman, but of the charms of a witch. Historical scholars question how the ignorant imagination of the Dark Ages distorted the poet Virgil into a magician. [Virgil is Dante's primary guide in the *Divine Comedy*.] One answer to the question, possibly, is that he was one. Theologians and philosophers debate about the inspiration of scripture, but perhaps the most philosophical argument, for saying that certain scriptural sayings are inspired, is simply that they sound like it. The great lines of the poets are like landscapes or visions, but the same strange light can be found not only in the high places of poetry but also in quite obscure corners of prose.

I can only express what I mean by saying that it is the finite part of the image that really suggests infinity. Most worthy and serious people, instead of saying the spiritual place, would say the spiritual world. Some dismal and disgusting people, instead of saying the spiritual place, would say the spiritual plane. The immediate chill and disenchantment of this change is due to a vague but vivid sense that the spiritual thing has become less real. A world sounds like an astronomical diagram, and a plane sounds like a geometrical diagram. Both of these are abstractions, but a place is not an abstraction, but a reality. The spiritual thrill is all in the idea that the place is a place, however spiritual, that it is some strange city where the sky touches the earth, or where eternity contrives to live on: the borderland of time and space.

In the mind of man, if not in the nature of things, there seems to be some connection between concentration and reality. When we want to ask, in natural language, whether a thing really exists or not, we ask if it is really "there" or not. We say "there," even if we do not clearly understand where. A man cannot enter a house by five doors at once; he might do it if he were in an atmosphere. But he does not want to be in an atmosphere. He has a stubborn subconscious belief that an animal is greater than an atmosphere. As a thing rises in the scale of things, it tends to localize and even narrow its natural functions. A man cannot absorb his sustenance through all his pores like a sponge or some low sea organisms; he cannot take in an atmosphere of beef, or an abstract essence of buns. Any buns thrown at him, as at the bear at the zoo, must be projected with such skill as to hit a particular hole in his head. In nature, in a sense, there is choice even before there is will. The plant or bulb narrows itself and pierces at one place rather than at another and all growth is a pattern of such green wedges. But however it be with these lower things, there has always been this spear-like selection and concentration in man's conception of higher things. Compared with that, there is something not only vague but vulgar in most of the talk about infinity. The pantheist is right up to a certain point, but so is the sponge.

Both vitally and verbally, this infinity is the enemy of all that is fine. Such philological points are sometimes more than pedantries or mere puns. And it is more than a pedantic pun to say that most things that are fine are finite. We testify to it when we talk of a beautiful thing having refinement or having finish. It is brought to an end like the blade of a beautiful sword, not only to its end in the sense of its cessation but to its end in the sense of its aim. All fine things are in this sense finished, even when they are eternal.

Poetry is committed to this concentration fully as much as religion: fairyland has always been as local, one might say as parochial, as Heaven. And if religion were removed tomorrow the poets would only begin to act as the pagans acted. They would begin to say "Lo, here," and "Lo, there," from the incurable itch of the idea that something must be somewhere, and not merely anywhere. Even if it were in some sense found to be in everything, it would still be in everything and not merely in all.

X

Sex

Rome rose at the expense of her Greek teachers largely because she did not entirely consent to be taught [their] tricks. She had a much more decent tradition; but she ultimately suffered from the same fallacy in her religious tradition; which was necessarily in no small degree the heathen tradition of nature worship. What was the matter with the whole heathen civilization was that there was nothing for the mass of men in the way of mysticism, except that concerned with the mystery of the nameless forces of nature, such as sex and growth and death. In the Roman Empire also, long before the end, we find nature-worship inevitably producing things that are against nature. Cases like that of Nero have passed into a proverb when Sadism sat on a throne brazen in the broad daylight. But the truth I mean is something much more subtle and universal than a conventional catalogue of atrocities. What had happened to the human imagination, as a whole, was that the whole world was colored by dangerous and rapidly deteriorating passions; by natural passions becoming unnatural passions. Thus the effect of treating sex as only one innocent natural thing was that every other innocent natural thing became soaked and sodden with sex. For sex cannot be admitted to a mere equality among elementary emotions or experiences like eating and sleeping. The moment sex ceases to be a servant it becomes a tyrant. There is something dangerous and disproportionate in its place in human nature, for whatever reason; and it does really need a special purification and dedication. The modern talk about sex being free like any other sense, about the body being beautiful like any tree or flower, is either a description of the Garden of Eden or a piece of thoroughly bad psychology, of which the world grew weary two thousand years ago.

Y

Yes

The fact that Thomism is the philosophy of common sense is itself a matter of common sense. Yet it wants a word of explanation, because we have so long taken such matters in a very uncommon sense. . . .

To this question "Is there anything?" St. Thomas begins by answering "Yes"; if he began by answering "No," it would not be the beginning, but the end. That is what some of us call common sense. Either there is no philosophy, no philosophers, no thinkers, no thought, no anything; or else there is a real bridge between the mind and reality. But he is actually less exacting than many thinkers, much less so than most rationalist and materialist thinkers, as to what that first step involves; he is content, as we shall see, to say that it involves the recognition of *Ens* or Being as something definitely beyond ourselves. *Ens* is *Ens*: Eggs are eggs, and it is not tenable that all eggs were found in a mare's nest.

Needless to say, I am not so silly as to suggest that all the writings of St. Thomas are simple and straight-forward; in the sense of being easy to understand. There are passages I do not in the least understand myself; there are passages that puzzle much more learned and logical philosophers than I am; there

are passages about which the greatest Thomists still
differ and dispute. But that is a question of a thing
being hard to read or understand: not hard to accept
when understood. That is a mere matter of "The Cat
sat on the Mat" being written in Chinese characters: or
"Mary had a Little Lamb" in Egyptian hieroglyphics.
The only point I am stressing here is that Aquinas is
almost always on the side of simplicity, and supports
the ordinary man's acceptance of ordinary truisms.
For instance, one of the most obscure passages, in my
very inadequate judgment, is that in which he explains
how the mind is certain of an external object and not
merely of an impression of that object; and yet apparently reaches it through a concept, though not merely
through an impression. But the only point here is that
he does explain that the mind is certain of an external
object. It is enough for this purpose that his conclusion
is what is called the conclusion of common sense; that
it is his purpose to justify common sense; even though
he justifies it in a passage which happens to be one of
rather uncommon subtlety. The problem of later philosophers is that their conclusion is as dark as their
demonstration; or that they bring out a result of which
the result is chaos.

Unfortunately, between the man in the street and
the Angel of the Schools, there stands at this moment a
very high brick wall, with spikes on the top, separating
two men who in many ways stand for the same thing.
The wall is almost a historical accident; at least it was
built a very long time ago, for reasons that need not
affect the needs of normal men today; least of all the
greatest need of normal men; which is for a normal
philosophy. The first difficulty is merely a difference
of form; not in the medieval but in the modern sense.

There is first a simple obstacle of language; there is
then a rather more subtle obstacle of logical method.
But the language itself counts for a great deal; even
when it is translated, it is still a foreign language; and
it is, like other foreign languages, very often translated
wrong. As with every other literature from another
age or country, it carried with it an atmosphere which
is beyond the mere translation of words, as they are
translated in a traveler's phrase-book. For instance, the
whole system of St. Thomas hangs on one huge and
yet simple idea; which does actually cover everything
there is, and even everything that could possibly be.
He represents this cosmic conception by the word *Ens*;
and anybody who can read any Latin at all, however
rudely, feels it to be the apt and fitting word; exactly as
he feels it in a French word in a piece of good French
prose. It ought to be a matter of logic; but it is also a
matter of language.

Unfortunately there is no satisfying translation
of the word *Ens*. The difficulty is rather verbal than
logical, but it is practical. I mean that when the trans-
lator says in English "being," we are aware of a rather
different atmosphere. Atmosphere ought not to affect
these absolutes of the intellect; but it does. The new
psychologists, who are almost eagerly at war with reason, never tire of telling us that the very terms we use
are colored by our subconsciousness, with something
we meant to exclude from our consciousness. And one
need not be so idealistically irrational as a modern psy-
chologist, in order to admit that the very shape and
sound of words do make a difference, even in the baldest prose, as they do in the most beautiful poetry. We
cannot quite prevent the imagination from remember-
ing irrelevant associations even in the abstract sciences

like mathematics. . . . Now it unfortunately happens
that the word "being," as it comes to a modern English-
man, through modern associations, has a sort of hazy
atmosphere that is not in the short and sharp Latin
word. Perhaps it reminds him of fantastic professors
in fiction, who wave their hands and say, "Thus do
we mount to the ineffable heights of pure and radiant
Being:" or, worse still, of actual professors in real life,
who say, "All Being is Becoming; and is but the evolution of Not-Being by the law of its Being." Perhaps it
only reminds him of romantic rhapsodies in old love
stories; "Beautiful and adorable being, light and breath
of my very being." Anyhow it has a wild and woolly
sort of sound; as if only very vague people used it; or
as if it might mean all sorts of different things.

Now the Latin word *Ens* has a sound like the
English word End. It is final and even abrupt; it is nothing except itself. There was once a silly gibe against
Scholastics like Aquinas, that they discussed whether
angels could stand on the point of a needle. It is at least
certain that this first word of Aquinas is as sharp as the
point of a pin. For that also is, in an almost ideal sense,
an End. But when we say that St. Thomas Aquinas is
concerned fundamentally with the idea of Being, we
must not admit any of the cloudier generalizations
that we may have grown used to, or even grown tired
of, in the sort of idealistic writing that is rather rhetoric than philosophy. Rhetoric is a very fine thing in
its place, as a medieval scholar would have willingly
agreed, as he taught it along with logic in the schools;
but St. Thomas Aquinas himself is not at all rhetorical. Perhaps he is hardly even sufficiently rhetorical.
There are any number of purple patches in Augustine;
but there are no purple patches in Aquinas. He did on

certain definite occasions drop into poetry; but he very seldom dropped into oratory. And so little was he in touch with some modern tendencies, that whenever he did write poetry, he actually put it into poems. There is another side to this, to be noted later. He very specially possessed the philosophy that inspires poetry; as he did so largely inspire Dante's poetry. And poetry without philosophy has only inspiration, or, in vulgar language, only wind. He had, so to speak, the imagination without the imagery. And even this is perhaps too sweeping. There is an image of his, that is true poetry as well as true philosophy; about the tree of life bowing down with a huge humility, because of the very load of its living fruitfulness; a thing Dante might have described so as to overwhelm us with the tremendous twilight and almost drug us with the divine fruit. But normally, we may say that his words are brief even when his books are long. I have taken the example of the word *Ens* precisely because it is one of the cases in which Latin is plainer than plain English. And his style, unlike that of St. Augustine and many Catholic Doctors, is always a penny plain rather than two pence colored. It is often difficult to understand, simply because the subjects are so difficult that hardly any mind, except one like his own, can fully understand them. But he never darkens it by using words without knowledge, or even more legitimately, by using words belonging only to imagination or intuition. So far as his method is concerned, he is perhaps the one real Rationalist among all the children of men.

Z

Zion

Jerusalem might be called a city of staircases. Many streets are steep and most actually cut into steps. It is, I believe, an element in the controversy about the cave at Bethlehem traditionally connected with the Nativity that the skeptics doubt whether any beasts of burden could have entered a stable that has to be reached by such steps. And indeed to any one in a modern city like London or Liverpool it may well appear odd, like a cab-horse climbing a ladder. But as a matter of fact, if the asses and goats of Jerusalem could not go up and downstairs, they could not go anywhere. However this may be, I mention the matter here merely as adding another touch to that angular profile which is the impression involved here. Strangely enough, there is something that leads up to this impression even in the labyrinth of mountains through which the road winds its way to the city. The hills around Jerusalem are themselves often hewn out in terraces, like a huge stairway. This is mostly for the practical and indeed profitable purpose of vineyards; and serves for a reminder that this ancient seat of civilization has not lost the tradition of the mercy and the glory of the vine. But in outline such a mountain looks much like the mountain of Purgatory that Dante saw in his vision, lifted in terraces,

like titanic steps up to God. And indeed this shape also
is symbolic; as symbolic as the pointed profile of the
Holy City. For a creed is like a ladder, while an evolution is only like a slope. A spiritual and social evolution
is generally a pretty slippery slope; a miry slope where
it is very easy to slide down again.

Such is something like the sharp and even abrupt
impression produced by this mountain city; and especially by its wall with gates like a house with windows.
A gate, like a window, is primarily a picture-frame. The
pictures that are found within the frame are indeed
very various and sometimes very alien. Within this
frame-work are indeed to be found things entirely Asiatic, or entirely Muslim, or even entirely nomadic. But
Jerusalem itself is not nomadic. Nothing could be less
like a mere camp of tents pitched by Arabs. Nothing
could be less like the mere chaos of color in a temporary and tawdry bazaar. The Arabs are there and
the colors are there, and they make a glorious picture;
but the picture is in a Gothic frame, and is seen so to
speak through a Gothic window. And the meaning of
all this is the meaning of all windows, and especially
of Gothic windows. It is that even light itself is most
divine within limits; and that even the shining one is
most shining, when he takes upon himself a shape.

Such a system of walls and gates, like many other
things thought rude and primitive, is really very rationalistic. It turns the town, as it were, into a plan of
itself, and even into a guide to itself. This is especially
true, as may be suggested in a moment, regarding the
direction of the roads leading out of it. But anyhow,
a man must decide which way he will leave the city;
he cannot merely drift out of the city as he drifts out
of the modern cities through a litter of slums. And

there is no better way to get a preliminary plan of the city than to follow the wall and fix the gates in the memory. Suppose, for instance, that a man begins in the south with the Zion Gate, which bears the ancient name of Jerusalem. This, to begin with, will sharpen the medieval and even the Western impression first because it is here that he has the strongest sentiment of threading the narrow passages of a great castle; but also because the very name of the gate was given to this south-western hill by Godfrey and Tancred during the period of the Latin kingdom [after the First Crusade]. I believe it is one of the problems of the scholars why the Latin conquerors called this hill the Zion Hill, when the other is obviously the sacred hill. Jerusalem is traditionally divided into four hills, but for practical purposes into two; the lower eastern hill where stood the Temple, and now stands the great Mosque, and the western where is the citadel and the Zion Gate to the south of it. I know nothing of such questions; and I attach no importance to the notion that has crossed my own mind, and which I only mention in passing, for I have no doubt there are a hundred objections to it. But it is known that Zion or Sion was the old name of the place before it was stormed by David; and even afterwards the Jebusites [Canaanites who, according to the Old Testament, built Jerusalem], remained on this western hill, and some compromise seems to have been made with them. Is it conceivable, I wonder, that even in the twelfth century there lingered some local memory of what had once been a way of distinguishing Sion of the Jebusites from Salem of the Jews? The Zion Gate, however, is only a starting-point here; if we go south-eastward from it we descend a steep and rocky path, from which can be caught the first and finest vision of what stands on the other hill to the east. The great Mosque of Omar [opposite the southern courtyard of the Church of the Holy Sepulchre] stands up like a peacock, lustrous with mosaics that are like plumes of blue and green.

Scholars, I may say here, object to calling it the Mosque of Omar; on the petty and pedantic ground that it is not a mosque and was not built by Omar. But it is my fixed intention to call it the Mosque of Omar, and with ever renewed pertinacity to continue calling it the Mosque of Omar. I possess a special permit from the Grand Mufti to call it the Mosque of Omar. He is the head of the whole Muslim religion, and if he does not know, who does? He told me, in the beautiful French which matches his beautiful manners, that it really is not so ridiculous after all to call the place the Mosque of Omar, since the great Caliph desired and even designed such a building, though he did not build it. I suppose it is rather as if Solomon's Temple had been called David's Temple. Omar was a great man and the Mosque was a great work, and the two were telescoped together by the excellent common sense of vulgar tradition. There could not be a better example of that great truth for all travelers; that popular tradition is never so right as when it is wrong; and that pedantry is never so wrong as when it is right. And as for the other objection, that the Dome of the Rock (to give it its other name) is not actually used as a Mosque, I answer that Westminster Abbey is not used as an Abbey. But modern Englishmen would be much surprised if I were to refer to it as Westminster Church; to say nothing of the many modern Englishmen for whom it would be more suitable to call it Westminster Museum. And for whatever purposes the Muslims may actually use their great and glorious sanctuary, at least they have not allowed it to become the private house of a particular rich man. And that is what we have suffered to happen, if not to Westminster Abbey, at least to Welbeck Abbey.

The Mosque of Omar (I repeat firmly) stands on the great eastern plateau in place of the Temple; and the wall that runs round to it on the south side of the city contains only the Dung Gate, on which the fancy need not linger. All along outside this wall the ground falls away into the southern valley; and upon the dreary and stony steep opposite is the place called Acaldama. Wall and valley turn together round the corner of the great temple platform, and confronting the eastern wall, across the ravine, is the mighty wall of the Mount of Olives. On this side there are several gates now blocked up, of which the most famous, the Golden Gate, carries in its very uselessness a testimony to the fallen warriors of the cross. For there is a strange Muslim legend that through this gate, so solemnly sealed up, shall ride the Christian King who shall again rule in Jerusalem. In the middle of the square enclosure rises the great dark Dome of the Rock; and standing near it, a man may see for the first time in the distance, another dome. It lies away to the west, but a little to the north; and it is surmounted, not by a crescent but a cross. Many heroes and holy kings have desired to see this thing, and have not seen it.

It is very characteristic of the city, with its medieval medley and huddle of houses, that a man may first see the Church of the Holy Sepulchre which is in the west, by going as far as possible to the east. All the sights are glimpses; and things far can be visible and things near invisible. The traveler comes on the Muslim dome

round a corner; and he finds the Christian dome, as it
were, behind his own back. But if he goes on round the
wall to the north-east corner of the Court of the Temple, he will find the next entrance; the Gate of St. Stephen. On the slope outside, by a strange and suitable
coincidence, the loose stones which lie on every side
of the mountain city seemed to be heaped higher; and
across the valley on the skirts of the Mount of Olives
is the great gray olive of Gethsemane.

Sources

A From "Le Jongleur De Dieu," chapter 5 of *Saint Francis*.

B From "The God in the Cave," Part II, chapter 1 of *The Everlasting Man*.

C From "The World Inside Out," chapter 4 of *The Catholic Church and Conversion*.

D From "On the Alleged Optimism of Dickens," chapter 11 of *Charles Dickens*.

E From "The Case for the Ephemeral," chapter 1 of *All Things Considered*.

F From "The Mirror of Christ," chapter 8 of *Saint Francis*.

G From "The Riddles of the Gospel," Part II, chapter 2 of *The Everlasting Man*.

H From "Introductory Remarks on the Importance of Orthodoxy," chapter 1 of *Heretics*.

I From "The Maniac," chapter 2 of *Orthodoxy*.

J From "The Maid of Orleans," chapter 33 of *All Things Considered*.

K From "The Philosophy of Sight-seeing," chapter 4 of *The New Jerusalem*.

L From "On Lying in Bed," chapter 10 of *Tremendous Trifles*.

M From "The Problem of St. Francis," chapter 1 of *Saint Francis*.

N From "On the Negative Spirit," chapter 2 of *Heretics*.

O From "The Romance of Orthodoxy," chapter 8 of *Orthodoxy*.

P From "The Greatness of Chaucer," chapter 1 of *Chaucer*.

Q From "The Canterbury Tales," chapter 5 of *Chaucer*.

R From "God and Comparative Religion," chapter 4 of *The Everlasting Man*.

S From "The Suicide of Thought," chapter 3 of *Orthodoxy*.

T From "The Permanent Philosophy," chapter 7 of *St. Thomas Aquinas*.

U   From *An Outline of Christianity*, 1926, reprinted in *The Catholic Church and Conversion*.

V   From "Queen Victoria," chapter 17 of *Varied Types*.

W   From *The New Witness*, November 25, 1925, reprinted in *The Common Man*.

X   From "The World St. Francis Found," chapter 2 of *Saint Francis*.

Y   From "The Approach to Thomism," chapter 6 of *St. Thomas Aquinas*.

Z   From "The Gates of the City," chapter 3 of *The New Jerusalem*.

G. K. Chesterton (1874–1936) was a prolific writer, poet, and satirist; a powerful journalist; and one of the most respected Catholic authors of the twentieth century. He converted to Catholicism in 1922 at the age of forty-eight.

Chesterton's book *Orthodoxy* is one of the classics of Christian apologetics. His novel *The Man Who Was Thursday* probably influenced Franz Kafka, and his clerical detective Father Brown was featured in dozens of stories and is second only to Sherlock Holmes as the most loved amateur fictional sleuth in history. Chesterton lived in London.

Peter Kreeft is an internationally renowned Chesterton expert, and has been a professor of philosophy at Boston College since 1965.

AVE
AVE MARIA PRESS

Founded in 1865, Ave Maria Press,
a ministry of the Congregation of
Holy Cross, is a Catholic publishing
company that serves the spiritual and
formative needs of the Church and its
schools, institutions, and ministers;
Christian individuals and families; and
others seeking spiritual nourishment.

For a complete listing of titles from

Ave Maria Press

Sorin Books

Forest of Peace

Christian Classics

visit www.avemariapress.com

AVE Maria Press
Notre Dame, IN
A Ministry of the United States Province of Holy Cross